The Young Oxfor
Christmas Stories

The Young Oxford Book of
Christmas Stories

DENNIS PEPPER

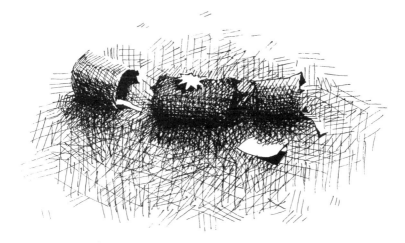

OXFORD
UNIVERSITY PRESS

OXFORD

UNIVERSITY PRESS

Great Clarendon Street, Oxford OX2 6DP

Oxford University Press is a department of the University of Oxford.
It furthers the University's objective of excellence in research, scholarship,
and education by publishing worldwide in

Oxford New York

Athens Auckland Bangkok Bogotá Buenos Aires
Cape Town Chennai Dar es Salaam Delhi Florence Hong Kong Istanbul
Karachi Kolkata Kuala Lumpur Madrid Melbourne Mexico City Mumbai
Nairobi Paris São Paulo Shanghai Singapore Taipei Tokyo Toronto Warsaw
with associated companies in Berlin Ibadan

Oxford is a registered trade mark of Oxford University Press
in the UK and in certain other countries

British Library Cataloguing in Publication Data available

ISBN 0-19-278168-5 (hardback)
ISBN 0-19-278169-3 (paperback)

1 3 5 7 9 10 8 6 4 2

Typeset by
Mary Tudge (Typesetting Services)

Printed in Great Britain by Biddles Ltd
www.biddles.co.uk

Contents

Introduction

Dear Oliver,

You wanted a book of Christmas stories that were *different*. Either that, or a computer game.

Well, try these. There are no shepherds watching, no reindeer, no Father Christmas ho-ho-hoing, no herald angels. Sleigh bells, like church bells, remain unrung. Of course, not everything you read at Christmas has to be about Christmas. Even Charles Dickens, who is often blamed for having started the sentimental season of feasting and jollity with his *A Christmas Carol*, included stories that had nothing whatever to do with Christmas in the annual Christmas numbers of magazines he edited. Many of them were straightforward ghost stories, and Christmas became for a time the main occasion for telling such stories.

There are ghosts in half a dozen of these stories. They are Christmas ghosts—or, at least, ghosts that appear for one reason or another at Christmas time—because this really is a book of Christmas stories. Many of the things we associated with Christmas *are* here: buying a Christmas present (even if you have to lie and cheat and resort to blackmail to do it); carol singing (though even the imperturbable Tucker can't extract a contribution from the miserly inhabitant of one old house); receiving presents (which in one story have been recycled over the years); the family Christmas dinner (which predictably descends into an acrimonious family row).

There is another side to this. We see Mary and Joseph on their way to that census count and even the three wise men, but not in a story about the Nativity. It is a different birth that is being celebrated in Gerald Kersh's story and we know, as the characters don't, how the story ends, but it is a celebration all the same. In another story a Jesuit

priest, an astrophysicist on a space ship exploring the after-effects of a star that had gone supernova, establishes without any shadow of doubt what it was that shone so brightly over Bethlehem 2000 years ago—and loses his faith. In 'The Night Is Freezing Fast' Alan and his grandpa, driving home through a raging blizzard, meet Death in the driveway. Although Alan doesn't understand what happens, we know that his grandpa has given him the most precious gift of all for Christmas.

Elsewhere there's Elizabeth, who hits her baby brother so hard she thinks she's killed him, as well she might have done, but who learns about love and forgiveness. And Jamie, who finally understands that Josef's death was all right. And the five-year-old Farrel boy, who made a secret promise and kept it. All of them stories to make you think what Christmas is really about.

So here it is: a collection of Christmas stories with a difference. Enjoy them.

Oh, yes: Happy Christmas.

Love from,

Dennis

The Imperturbable Tucker
A. M. Burrage

IT could only have happened in a large town parish, whose ill-defined boundaries were known only to the vicar and the parish clerk, if even to them. And it happened on Christmas Eve, which means that the weather was muggy and wet, and that everybody with any desire or pretensions to sing carols—and many who had neither—were out and after their neighbours' legal tender.

The official carol singers, comprising certain male voices from the church choir, led by Mr Thomas Tucker, were, of course, doing better business than their rivals.

The reasons for this were many and good. The noises they produced were less painful to sensitive ears. They had *locus standi*. And where Mr Tucker observed no symptoms of generosity he was able to plead that all the monies were to be handed direct to a most deserving cause.

Apart from the facts that he had a baritone voice of sorts, and could reach the compass of a sailor having teeth out without gas, there seemed no very good reason why Thomas Tucker should be a member of the church choir.

Many people questioned why he was, although the answer was quite simple. It was simply because he was a creature of habit and had been made to join the choir as a small boy. His mother had conveyed him to all the practices by the left ear—which even now protruded a little more than the right—until the habit was so engrafted on him that he could be trusted to go alone.

For similar reasons he was now a butcher. He had been apprenticed to the trade in days when his fancy had lightly turned to the High Seas and to deeds of doubtful ethics under a flag which he was wont to call the Jolly Ole Roger. He had become a full-blown butcher simply because everybody else connected with that particular shop had died, and because he had heard that the only pirates left were certain Asiatic gentlemen who lived principally on rats, birds' nests, and unwanted dogs.

He was not only a person with whom habit soon became unalterable nature, but one to whom nothing came amiss. He was phlegmatic as a waxwork figure, and people said that it was impossible to shock, surprise, or scare him. How true this may be the reader must presently judge for himself.

Tucker and his band of singers had been out some two hours ere they came to a curious old house, once of some pretensions, hiding away from its new and perky neighbours behind a red wall enclosing a bedraggled garden. Two or three members of the choir halted before the rusty gate and debated as to whether the house came within the parish boundary.

'Doesn't matter,' said Tucker. 'People who live in it won't know either.'

And he pushed open the creaking gate and led the procession up the path. They formed a semicircle in front of the hall door of the dingy old house that showed not a light anywhere.

'I b'lieve it's empty,' said the leading tenor.

'Soon see,' said Tucker. ' "Good King Wenceslas".'

They got as far as the good king's lavish order for pine logs, when they suddenly stopped, Tucker finishing the verse alone. No lights had appeared, and all except Tucker were convinced that they were wasting their breath on an empty house.

Hoarsely they pointed out this probability once more to Tucker, who had otherwise, from force of habit, gone through with the carol to the bitter end and possibly begun another.

'Soon see,' said Tucker. 'Wait a sec.'

He strode to the steps and walked up to the door. There was a great black handle which slipped back under pressure, and Tucker pushed the door open before him.

'Don't be a fool!' hissed a voice. 'You can't walk in.'

'I have,' said Tucker, and he closed the door behind him.

At first it seemed to him that the house really was empty. There were no lights in the front rooms, as he had already seen from without, and the place smelt of dust and decay. But nothing less than a complete inspection of the premises would satisfy him; and largesse would certainly be demanded of any human being.

He was on his way to the servants' quarters when he noticed that a door on his left was thinly framed by a bluish light stealing through its chinks. Tucker pushed open the door without knocking and entered the room beyond.

The room was small and almost devoid of furniture. It was lit by a candle which burned strangely, and gave the wan bluish light which had attracted him.

In a far corner a villainous-looking old man was on his knees before a great chest. The old man was clad in rags, and the wicked leering face above his dirty white beard would have inspired a medieval designer of gargoyles.

But in spite of his rags the chest was full of gold pieces which ran like sand through his long, crooked fingers, and chinked wickedly as they dropped. The scene was weird enough, and sufficiently awe-inspiring to appal the stoutest heart.

'Evenin',' said Tucker.

The old man's wicked eyes blazed at him.

'Stranger,' he said in deep, hollow tones, 'what do you here?'

'Collecting,' said Tucker. 'Ain't you heard the carol-singers?'

'No!'

'Ah, you ought to have been round in the front. Will you go round or shall I bring 'em in here?'

'Do you know whom you address?' cried the old man in an awful voice. 'I am Devloe, the miser.'

'Pleased to meet you,' said Tucker. 'Subscriptions, however small, are invited. You don't seem to have anything less than Jimmy O'Goblins in that box. So much the better.'

'You will get naught from me,' cried the old man angrily.

'I bet I do. Buck up. Then we'll sing to you. Will you have "Noel" or "Hark the Herald"?'

'The only music I delight in is the tinkling of these little coins which are my heart's blood to me.'

'Quite nice,' Tucker agreed, 'I wish I had a few of 'em. Come on. It's Christmas time, and this is a good cause.'

'Never,' cried the old man, 'have I ever given anything away.'

'Time you did, then,' said Tucker.

'This is tainted gold.'

'Can't help that,' said Tucker. 'We've got two company promoters in our congregation, and there'd be a row if the verger didn't pass 'em the plate.'

'Every penny of this was wrung from the poor—'

'And I bet it wanted some wringing,' said Tucker. 'You ought to see the money I've got out on my books.'

'Except what was stolen by violence.'

'Ah, that's easier,' said Tucker.

'I have committed bigamy, theft, arson, forgery.'

'Really,' said Tucker, faintly interested.

'And two murders!' thundered the old man.

'You have been a bit of a nib, haven't you?' said Tucker agreeably. 'But think what a comfort it will be to you to know that you've contributed—'

A look of hopelessness dawned in the old man's wicked eyes.

'Will nothing frighten you away from here?' he demanded.

'Not that I know of.'

'And you will not go?'

'Not until you've subscribed—'

The old man interrupted him with a loud groan.

'Take a coin, then,' he said resignedly. 'Stay, I will find you the smallest. Anything to get rid—'

'Hold hard,' said Tucker. 'You needn't be mean about it. Remember it's for an excellent cause.'

'What cause?'

'The Church Warming Fund,' said Tucker.

A terrible cry emanated from the top of the old man's beard. He dropped the lid of the chest and held it down as firmly as he could with his thin hands.

'Look here!' he exclaimed. 'There *are* limits, you know. I told you the kind of life I led. Well, I died years ago, and if you think I'm going to subscribe to any kind of *warming* fund—'

Words suddenly failed him, and so, seemingly, did everything else. The light and the apparition—for an apparition Tucker now knew it to be—vanished in a flash.

'There now!' Tucker murmured.

He lingered to strike a match and see if the treasure chest had also vanished. Finding that it had, he murmured, 'There's a pity!' and went out to rejoin his fellow carol-singers.

'Any luck?' someone shouted, as he reappeared.

Tucker shook his head.

'Found an old man, but I couldn't get nothing out of him.'

'Why didn't you tell 'im to go to blazes?' somebody demanded.

'Wasn't necessary,' said Tucker. 'Come on. Next house.'

Many Happy Reruns

Katherine Paterson

E LIZABETH wished Miss Violet would stop singing. She had a screechy voice that hurt Elizabeth's ears like the *wheee* when her mother would let the teakettle stay on too long. The song had gone on too long. Sunday School had gone on too long. And Miss Violet had gone on far too long. Elizabeth felt like saying 'Shut up' just like that, right in the middle of the class. Wouldn't everybody be surprised if she did that? Just 'Shut up.' She said it over again inside her head. Why couldn't kids say 'Shut up' to grown-ups? Grown-ups were always saying it to children. Maybe not 'Shut up', but 'Will you *please* be quiet while your mother is trying to rest?'

'Has everyone seen the manger scene in the big church?' Miss Violet had finally stopped singing and started teaching.

'Ye-es,' said all the children except Elizabeth, who was studying the crack in the wall above Miss Violet's head. If you took a crayon and put a thing with two points at the round part, it would look just like a snake getting ready to bite.

'And who remembers why Jesus was born?'

'To save us from our sins!' All the children yelled except Elizabeth.

'Elizabeth'—Miss Violet leaned over the picture she was holding of Baby Jesus in the manger—'Elizabeth, we're talking about something very important to all of us. Don't you want Jesus to save you from your sins?'

'Yes'm.' Except that Elizabeth was extremely fuzzy on just what sins she wished to be saved from. Was punching Willis Morgan in the stomach when he called you a dumdum a sin? She hardly thought so. Even God must know you couldn't help that. Was it a sin to wish that stupid baby would hurry up and be born so Aunt Gladys would go away and never come back again? How could it be? Was it a sin to hate Aunt Gladys? Probably. But it wasn't a sin she wanted to be saved from. No—sin was like killing somebody when you weren't even a policeman or a cowboy—like hating somebody for no reason.

She didn't hate Miss Violet. She didn't feel much of anything towards Miss Violet. Except for her singing, which was terrible, the rest of Miss Violet was all right. She was kind of like the church—very old and crumbly, mostly boring but not scary. It was probably because Miss Violet had always lived right next door to the church ever since she was Elizabeth's age and her father was the minister. He had died many years before Elizabeth was born. Most of the old houses on the block had long ago been bulldozed for stores or apartments, but Miss Violet wouldn't sell 'dear Poppa's manse'.

Elizabeth sighed. Her best friend Kimberly Wood stayed home all Sunday morning and watched TV. They had old movies and *Wonderama* with cartoons, Kimberly said. Why didn't Elizabeth's mother or father come and pick her up? Church was like a rerun of a dumb show you didn't like the first time, but at least there Elizabeth could sit squeezed between her parents and draw pictures on the backs of the pew envelopes. It was crazy. If you sat for the hour drawing on the backs of the envelopes, everyone would tell your parents afterwards what a wonderful little girl they had and weren't they proud. But if you tried to listen to all the preaching and praying and when you didn't understand something, just whisper a tiny little question, both your parents looked angry and said 'Shh!' and nobody said how good you were.

Elizabeth sighed again. Why didn't her mother and father pick her up?

But, of course, today her mother wouldn't come and get her. Her mother was in the hospital having that stupid baby. When Elizabeth had woken up this morning, neither her father nor her mother had been in their bed. There was just Aunt Gladys, grinning and clucking about. But she didn't grin when Elizabeth picked up her whole sunny-side egg with her fingers and ate it in one gulp. No, she didn't grin then, she yelped like Scooby-Doo when he saw a ghost. Elizabeth had to giggle when she remembered it.

Aunt Gladys was standing at the Sunday School door, waiting for Miss Violet to finish her prayer. She was staring right at Elizabeth. What could she have done wrong now? She hadn't seen Aunt Gladys for an hour.

'Elizabeth, you should bow your head and close your eyes during the prayer,' Aunt Gladys said as she helped Elizabeth put on her coat. 'Don't you know God wants us to worship him reverently?'

It occurred to Elizabeth that Aunt Gladys must also have forgotten to close her eyes during the prayer, and she was sorely tempted to say so, but 'Yes'm' was all she actually said.

'We can't stay for church this morning,' Aunt Gladys said as she took Elizabeth's hand. 'Your father may be trying to reach us.' After they crossed the first street, Elizabeth slipped her hand away and into her pocket and kept it there for the six long cold blocks to the tall skinny house where Elizabeth lived.

There wasn't even a decoration on the door. Elizabeth had seen a huge Santa Claus in the dime store last week, but she couldn't persuade Aunt Gladys to buy it. Santa Claus probably wouldn't come this year. When she'd told her mother she wanted a 'Baby Alive' just as they advertised on TV, her mother had laughed and said, 'Oh, we'll have a baby alive all right. That will be enough diapers for this Christmas.' So when her father had asked her if she'd rather have a baby brother or a baby sister for Christmas, she'd said right out, 'I'd rather have a two-wheeler with a banana seat.' He'd laughed as though he thought she was kidding, but she wasn't kidding a bit. She didn't want some dumb baby for a Christmas present. They'd probably stop having Christmas ever again. Every year it would be the baby's birthday, and they'd all be so busy buying it presents and making it a cake that they wouldn't even remember to have Christmas.

The phone was ringing when they opened the door. Elizabeth ran through the hall as fast as she could to get there first, but Aunt Gladys took the receiver right out of her hand.

'Ohhh, Richard, that's *lovely*. Now isn't that just the right weight? A perfect baby.' Elizabeth was jumping up and down. She thought she would scream if Aunt Gladys didn't shut up and give her the phone back. 'And how is Linda? . . . Well, that's quite natural. I know you're thrilled . . . What's the name, now?'

Elizabeth couldn't keep still any longer. 'Give it to me! Give it to me! I gotta talk to Daddy.'

But Aunt Gladys acted as though she didn't hear. She began to give Elizabeth's father a long list of relatives that he ought to call right away.

'Give it to me!' Elizabeth begged.

Aunt Gladys put her hand over the mouth of the receiver. 'Be quiet for one minute, please, Elizabeth. Oh, I think that's a mistake, Richard. You said yourself she was worn out. You tell her to take it easy and take all the time she needs to build up her strength. We'll do just fine here . . .'

Elizabeth went up the stairs to her room. The bed with the pink spread was really hers, but now Aunt Gladys was sleeping in it and Elizabeth had to use the cot. She plopped down on the cot. Never before in her life had she been so angry that she couldn't even cry. She picked up Ernie and punched him hard in the stomach. He smiled his shoe-button smile. There was a hole behind his ear, and some of his stuffing was coming out. She tried to push it back in, but it crumbled up in her hand. 'Shut up,' she said to Ernie, but he just kept on smiling. She stuck her fingers into the hole and tore it a little more. It tore neatly with a rip-rip-rip kind of sound, so she kept on tearing.

The first thing Aunt Gladys said to her father when he came home that evening was that Elizabeth had 'maliciously destroyed' her toy dog and strewn the stuffings all over the bed. Elizabeth wasn't familiar with the word 'maliciously', but it sounded as though it ought not to rhyme with 'deliciously'. Her father looked hurt and disappointed and tired, which made Elizabeth sorry. Perhaps it was a sin to kill a stuffed dog. At any rate she felt bad, looking at him in the wastebasket, his smile still sewn onto a funny flat face.

But her father was not angry. He sat in his big brown chair and pulled Elizabeth up into his lap. She snuggled up under his chin, which was all prickly.

'You tickle, Daddy.'

'No time to shave this morning, Snicklefritz.' He rubbed his chin hard against her cheek to tease her. Elizabeth giggled. 'Did Aunt Gladys tell you about your new brother?'

Elizabeth shook her head. Of course, Aunt Gladys had, but she wanted to hear it from her daddy. She sighed happily as he began to tell her the story of how he and Mommy had rushed out that morning when the whole city was still asleep . . . Oh, yes, of course the firemen and policemen and doctors and nurses and the people at the TV station were awake.

'How about Jesus?'

'No, Jesus wasn't asleep. He was watching over you and Mommy and the baby about to be born.'

'And you, too?'

'Me, too, Snicklefritz.'

Though why anyone as big as Daddy needed Jesus to look after him was more than Elizabeth could understand.

Her father went on with the story—how baby Joshua came yelling into the world—and how he and Mommy decided to call him Joshua out of the Bible because it means 'God is deliverance', which is the same thing that 'Jesus' means and Joshua and Jesus would have almost the same birthday.

And then he told her that Joshua weighed seven pounds, eight ounces . . . but why was that important? The important thing was that her mother was going to come home on Christmas Eve—'Yes, Gladys, the doctor is sure it's all right'—so they would all be together for Christmas.

Elizabeth could have died of joy on the spot. Her mother coming home—Aunt Gladys would go away, and then the three of them could be happy again just as they used to be.

On Christmas Eve, Elizabeth's mother came as her father had promised, but it was not the same. In the first place, Aunt Gladys did not leave. And in the second place, everyone was always kitchy-cooing over this baby.

Elizabeth could hardly stand it. He wasn't even cute. He was bald, and his face was the colour of a cherry cough drop when he cried—which was most of the time. Her mother let her sit in the brown chair and hold him, but Joshua screamed right in her face, and Elizabeth knew he hated her even if she was his sister. She didn't want to hold him any more. He cried too much. She turned on the TV set, but she could still hear him.

'Maybe he's not getting enough milk!' Aunt Gladys would rush out to fix a bottle, and then she and Elizabeth's mother would have a fight because Elizabeth's mother wanted to feed him all by herself. 'And for goodness' sake, Gladys, the doctor said to hold off on formula. *Please* I do know what I'm doing.'

Grown-ups might call it a disagreement, but Elizabeth could recognize a fight when she heard one. It made her stomach knot up to see her mother angry but still trying to be nice. There was nothing to do but sit around and listen to the grown-ups fuss and hear the baby cry. She didn't want to watch TV. She wanted to decorate the Christmas tree, but her mother said, 'Wait for Daddy, please, sweetie,' and Elizabeth didn't want to ask Aunt Gladys to help. Then she had a marvellous idea. She'd do it all by herself and surprise everyone. All anyone had said lately was what a big girl she had to be now that there was to be a new baby around. 'I'm sure you're going to be a real helper for your mother.' That's what Miss Violet had said on Sunday.

She even knew where in the attic the Christmas box was kept. It was too heavy for her, but that was all right. She could carry a few things down at a time. On the first trip she carried the lights and one box of balls. The balls were tricky. She had to keep sliding them back so they wouldn't fall off the top of the pile, but she managed. Proudly she set the load down under the tree and went back for more.

She passed her mother carrying Joshua in the upstairs hall. 'What are you doing, sweetie?' she asked, but Elizabeth could see that her eyes were looking that funny way that meant she wasn't really paying attention. 'Nothing,' Elizabeth answered, and her mother smiled and said, 'Fine.' Then her mother carried Joshua to the little room Daddy had fixed up and put him back to bed. When she came out again, she smiled vaguely at Elizabeth and went into her own room and lay down. Good. She'd go to sleep, and when she woke up, Elizabeth would have the tree all beautiful for her.

The last load was the heaviest. Elizabeth started to divide it and come back for the manger scene, but it was a long trip, and she was in a hurry, so she put the shoe box with the manger scene on top of everything else and started slowly down the two flights of stairs to the living room. She was almost to the landing . . . Careful, careful, just a little further.

'Elizabeth. What are you doing?'

Elizabeth jerked upright, and the shoe box slid off, turned in the air, and crashed at the bottom of the stairs.

'Oh, no!' Aunt Gladys cried. Then she fell to her knees and unwrapped the tissue paper, revealing a shattered shepherd. 'It's the porcelain Nativity that my father brought from Germany before I was born. I've loved it ever since I was a tiny child. And now—now'

Elizabeth didn't know what to do. She just stood there with her arms full of boxes of balls and tinsel. She hoped the Baby Jesus wasn't broken. She loved the way its eyes were closed with little tiny painted lashes. Jesus did *too* sleep.

'Can't you even say you're sorry? Do you know what you've done?' Aunt Gladys started up the stairs towards Elizabeth.

Elizabeth was scared. She didn't want Aunt Gladys to get her. She threw down the rest of the boxes as hard as she could and ran up the stairs. Her mother was standing at the railing, blocking the way to Elizabeth's own room, so she ran to the baby's room, slammed the door, and leaned against it. The button was right there in the lock on the inside, so she punched it in. Just in time, too, because they were both there, her mother and Aunt Gladys, banging on the door and yelling at her to let them in.

'We've got to get in there, Linda. There's no telling what she might do. The child might do something malicious.'

'Gladys!'

'I mean it, Linda. You should have seen the expression on her face when she threw those boxes at me.'

'Elizabeth, sweetie, let Mommy in.'

'Let us in, Elizabeth. Right this minute!'

The baby began to scream. 'Shut up!' yelled Elizabeth. 'Shut up.' It seemed to her that the baby was yelling even louder.

'What is she doing to the baby? Linda, you've got to get someone—the fire department—the police—someone! She might hurt him.'

'Nonsense, Gladys. Elizabeth . . .'

Elizabeth went over to the crib. Joshua's face was all red and all mouth. 'Shut up,' she said quietly, but she meant it. 'If you don't shut up this minute, I'm going to smack you to kingdom come.'

'Well, if you won't call someone, I will.'

'Joshua, if you don't shut up, Aunt Gladys will call the police, and I'll be in jail for Christmas.' Elizabeth was desperate. 'Shut up, Joshua. I mean it. Shut up this minute.'

'I'm going to call, Linda. Right this minute . . .'

'Gladys, *please* . . .'

Elizabeth lifted her hand over the baby and smacked hard, really hard. Harder than she'd ever punched Willis Morgan, harder than she'd ever hit anybody in the world. For a moment there was dead silence.

I killed him, thought Elizabeth, I killed my own brother. She raced to the window, unlocked it, then shoved it up—just as Daddy had shown her at the fire drill. She threw out the rope fire escape and climbed to the ground. It didn't even matter that she only had a sweater on; she was running too hard to notice. She had to get hold of Jesus at once. If you got put in jail for locking a door, what happened if you killed your own brother? She ran as fast as she could, and when she got to the church door, she yanked on the big handle with all her might. It was locked.

'Jesus,' Elizabeth yelled. 'Let me in. You gotta help me.' She began beating on the door with both her fists. Her teeth were rattling in her head. 'Jesus, please, please! You gotta help me.'

'Elizabeth?' It was Miss Violet. She had on an old purple sweater,

and the front part of her hair was in paper curlers. 'Elizabeth, what in the world are you doing here?' Elizabeth threw her arms around the wrinkled old neck. 'Oh, Miss Violet! You gotta help me find Jesus. You gotta help me.'

Miss Violet took Elizabeth's hand and led her to her own house, where the door stood open. 'You scared me out of my wits with all that crying. What are you doing here, anyway, all by yourself with no coat on, even?'

'I killed baby Joshua, Miss Violet. I didn't mean to, but he wouldn't stop screaming and they were going to take me to jail. You gotta tell Jesus to help me. He won't listen to me now. He hates me.'

'There, there, just a minute.' Miss Violet sat down in her old rocker—the one that had once been 'Poppa's chair'—and pulled the sobbing Elizabeth into her lap. 'Why don't you tell me what happened.' So Elizabeth told her, and Miss Violet didn't interrupt; she didn't fuss; she didn't smile. She just stroked Elizabeth's hair and rocked.

'So what do you want Jesus to do, Elizabeth?' she asked when Elizabeth had finished all the crying she was able to do.

There was a long silence. 'He can't make the baby alive again, can he?'

'I gave up a long time ago weighing what he could or couldn't do, Elizabeth.'

'That's the main thing.' Elizabeth twisted her finger in a hole in Miss Violet's sweater.

'Is that all?'

'He can't save me, can he?'

'What do you mean, Elizabeth?'

'I'm—I'm malicious. That means nobody could save me from my sins.'

Miss Violet tightened her arms about Elizabeth. She smelled like the sachet in Mommy's sweater drawer. Her chin was all soft, not prickly like Daddy's. Elizabeth began to cry once more. She would never be able to sit on her father's lap and be called Snicklefritz again.

'Go to Hell.' That's what Jesus would say, and her daddy would look sad and tired, but he wouldn't be able to help her. The tall black gates yawned open before her. Daddy might even hate her, too. Just like Jesus did for killing her little brother. And her mother? Her mother would be so lonely with no more children in the world . . .

Suddenly Elizabeth sat up and looked hard at Miss Violet. 'Why are *you* crying, Miss Violet? You didn't do anything bad.'

'Because'—Miss Violet's voice was pinched and tiny—'because I love you very much.'

Elizabeth snuffled loudly, and then she sat quietly listening to the creak-creak-creak of Poppa's rocker and Miss Violet's sniffles. Elizabeth couldn't remember ever having seen a grown-up cry before—sometimes on TV but never really and truly. And Miss Violet hadn't done *anything* bad. . . A tiny light began to grow in her, deep down inside.

'Does Jesus ever cry, Miss Violet?'

'Yes.' Miss Violet retrieved a lace-edged handkerchief from her sweater pocket and dabbed her eyes and nose. 'Yes, it says so in the Bible. It says, "Jesus wept."'

'That's in the Bible?'

Miss Violet nodded.

'Good,' said Elizabeth, feeling the light grow inside her, and hearing finally, to her great joy, the black iron gates clang shut. 'That is really good to know.'

When Aunt Gladys appeared at Miss Violet's door, her face was red and puffy as if she, too, had been crying.

She dropped to her knees and put her arms around Elizabeth. 'Oh, you crazy child, you had us frantic.' Then she seemed to remember where she was and stood up and thanked Miss Violet. 'You can't imagine how I felt. I was terrified. Linda finally got into the room with a screwdriver. There was the baby, screaming his little head off, and nothing left of Elizabeth except an open second-storey window. It's a mercy she didn't kill herself climbing out. We couldn't imagine where she'd gone—no coat as you see.' Aunt Gladys patted the coat she had brought along. 'It was getting dark. We couldn't reach her father.' Aunt Gladys blew her nose. 'What a relief to get your call. You can't imagine . . . Her poor mother was panicked, and I—I—it was all my fault. I'm just too old. I just don't know how to deal with children any more. I wanted to help. I really thought I could help, but it would have been far better if I had never c—'

'Aunt Gladys. Will you *please* be quiet for one minute?' Elizabeth stuck her arms up, and Aunt Gladys, her mouth still open, helped her put on her coat. Then Elizabeth took Aunt Gladys's hand. 'We gotta go home now, Miss Violet. Tell Jesus thank you, and happy birthday.'

'You tell him yourself, Elizabeth. He's listening.'

Elizabeth grinned. 'Happy birthday, Jesus,' she said softly. 'And many happy reruns of the day.'

The Night Is Freezing Fast
Thomas F. Monteleone

IT started with a curse—albeit a mild one.

'Oh *damn*!' cried Grandma from the kitchen. When ten-year-old Alan heard her cursing, he knew she was serious.

Grandpa eased the Dubuque newspaper down from his face, and spoke to her. 'What's the matter?'

'I ran out of shortnin' for this cake . . . and if you want a nice dessert for Christmas dinner, you'll get yourself into town and get me some more.'

'But it's a *blizzard* goin' on out there!' said Grandpa.

Grandma said nothing. Grandpa just sighed as he dropped his paper, shuffled across the room to the foyer closet.

Alan watched him open the door and pull out snow-boots, a beat-up corduroy hat, and a Mackinaw jacket of red and black plaid. He turned and looked wistfully at Alan, who was sitting in on the floor half-watching a football game.

'Want to take a ride, Alan?'

'Into town?'

'Yep. 'Fraid so.'

'In the blizzard?'

Grandpa sighed, stole a look towards the kitchen. 'Yep.'

'Yeah! That'll be *great* fun,' he said.

Alan ran to the closet and pulled on the heavy, rubber-coated boots, a knit watch-cap, and scarf. Then he shook into the goose down parka his mom had ordered from the L.L. Bean mail-order place. It was so *different* out here in Iowa.

'Forty-two years with that woman and I don't know how she figures she can . . .'

Grandpa had just closed the door to the mud-porch behind them. He was muttering as he faced into the stinging slap of the December wind, the bite of the ice-hard snowflakes attacking his cheeks. Alan heard on the radio that there would be roof-high drifts by morning if it kept up like this.

Grandpa stepped down to the path shovelled towards the garage. It was already starting to fill in and would need some new digging out pretty soon.

The hypnotic effect of the snow fascinated Alan. 'Do you get storms like this all the time, Grandpa?'

''Bout once a month this bad.' Grandpa reached the garage door, threw it up along its spring-loaded tracks. He shook his head and shivered from the wind-chill. 'I don't know about you, but *I'd* rather be with your mom and dad, takin' that cruise right about now.'

'No way! This is going to be the first *real* Christmas I ever had!'

'Why? Because it's a *white* one?' Grandpa chuckled as he opened the door of the 4-wheel-drive Scout, climbed in.

'Sure,' said Alan. 'Haven't you ever heard that song?'

Grandpa smiled. 'Oh, I think I've heard it a time or two . . .'

'Well, that's what I mean. It *never* seems like Christmas in L.A.— even when it *is* Christmas!' Alan jumped into the Scout and slammed the door. The blizzard awaited them.

Grandpa eased the Scout from the driveway to Route 14A. Alan looked out across the flat landscape of the other farms in the distance, and felt disoriented. He could not tell where the snowy land stopped and the white of the sky began. When the Scout lurched forward out onto the main road it looked like they were constantly driving smack into a white sheet of paper, a white nothingness.

It was scary, thought Alan. Just as scary as driving into a pitch-black night.

'Oh, she picked a fine time to run out of something for that danged cake! Look at it, Alan. It's goin' to be a regular *white-out*, is what it is.'

Alan nodded. 'How do you know where you're going, Grandpa?'

Grandpa harrumphed. 'Been on this road a million times, boy. Lived here all my life! I'm not about to get lost. But my God, it's *cold* out here! Hope this heater gets going pretty soon . . .'

They drove on in silence except for the scrunch of the tyres on the packed snow and *thunk-thunk* of the wiper blades trying to move off the hard new flakes that pelted the glass. The heater still pumped chilly air into the cab and Alan's breath was almost freezing as it came out of his mouth.

He imagined that they were explorers on a far-away planet—an alien world of ice and eternally freezing winds. It was an instantaneous, catapulting adventure of the type only possible in the minds of imaginative ten year olds. There were creatures out in the blizzard—great white hulking things. Pale, reptilian, evil-eyed things. Alan squinted through the windshield, ready in his gun-turret if one turned on them. He would blast it with his laser-cannons . . .

'What in *heck*?' muttered Grandpa.

Abruptly, Alan was out of his fantasy-world as he stared past the flicking windshield wipers. There was a dark shape standing in the centre of the white nothingness. As the Scout advanced along the invisible road, drawing closer to the contrasted object, it became clearer, more distinct.

It was a man. He was standing by what must be the roadside, waving a gloved hand at Grandpa.

Braking easily, Grandpa stopped the Scout and reached across to unlock the door. The blizzard rushed in ahead of the stranger, slicing through Alan's clothes like a cold knife. 'Where you headed?!' cried Grandpa over the wind. 'I'm going as far as town . . .'

'That'll do,' said the stranger.

Alan caught a glimpse of him as he pushed into the back seat. He was wearing a thin coat that seemed to hang on him like a scarecrow's rags. He had a black scarf wrapped tight around his neck and a dark blue ski mask that covered his face under a floppy-brimmed old hat. Alan didn't like that—not being able to see the stranger's face.

'Cold as hell out there!' said the man as he smacked his gloved hands together. He laughed to himself, then: 'Now there's a funny expression for you, ain't it? "Cold as hell." Don't make much sense, does it? But people still say it, don't they?'

'I guess they do,' said Grandpa as he slipped the Scout into gear and started off again. Alan looked at the old man, who looked like an older version of his father, and thought he saw an expression of concern, if not apprehension, forming on the lined face.

'It's not so funny, though . . .' said the stranger, his voice lowering a bit. 'Everybody figures hell to be this *hot* place, but it don't *have* to be, you know?'

'Never really thought about it much,' said Grandpa, jiggling with the heater controls. It was so cold, thought Alan. It just didn't seem to want to work.

Alan shivered, uncertain whether or not it was from the lack of heat, or the words, the voice of the stranger.

'Matter of fact, it makes more sense to think of hell as full of all kinds of *different* pain. I mean, fire is so unimaginative, don't you think? Now, *cold* . . . something as cold as that wind out there could be just as bad, right?' The man in the back seat chuckled softly beneath the cover of the ski mask. Alan didn't like that sound.

Grandpa cleared his throat and faked a cough. 'I don't think I've really thought much about that either,' he said as he appeared to be concentrating on the snow-covered road ahead. Alan looked at his grandfather's face and could see the unsteadiness in the old man's eyes. It was the look of fear, slowly building.

'Maybe you should . . .' said the stranger.

'Why?' said Alan. 'What do you mean?'

'It stands to reason that a demon would be comfortable in any kind of element—as long as it's harsh, as long as it's cruel.'

Alan tried to clear his throat and failed. Something was stuck down there, even when he swallowed.

The stranger chuckled again. ''Course, I'm getting off the track . . . we were talking about figures of speech, weren't we?'

'You're the one doing all the talking, mister,' said Grandpa.

The stranger nodded. 'Actually, a more appropriate expression would be "cold as the *grave*" . . .'

'It's not *this* cold under the ground,' said Alan defensively.

'Now, how would *you* know?' asked the stranger slowly. 'You've never been in the grave . . . not *yet*, anyway.'

'That's enough of that silly talk, mister!' said Grandpa. His voice was hard-sounding, but Alan detected fear beneath the thin layer of his words.

Alan looked from his grandfather to the stranger. As his eyes locked in with those behind the ski mask, Alan felt an ice-pick touch the tip of his spine. There was something about the stranger's eyes, something dark which seemed to lurch and caper violently behind them.

A dark chuckle came from the back seat.

'Silly talk? *Silly?*' asked the stranger. 'Now what's silly and what's serious in the world today? Who can *tell* any more? Missiles and summit conferences! Vampires and garlic! Famine and epidemics! Full moons and maniacs!'

The words rattled out of the dark man and chilled Alan more deeply than the cold blast of the heater fan. He looked away and tried to stop the shiver which raced up and down his back-bone.

'Where'd you say you was goin', mister?' asked Grandpa as he slowly eased off the gas-pedal.

'I didn't say.'

'Well, how about sayin'—right now.'

'Do I detect hostility in your voice, sir? Or is it something else?' Again came the deep-throated, whispery chuckle.

Alan kept his gaze upon the white-on-white panorama ahead. But he was listening to every word being exchanged between the dark stranger and his grandfather, who was suddenly assuming the proportions of a champion. He listened but he could not turn around, he could not look back. There was a fear gripping him now. It was a gnarled spindly claw reaching up for him, out of the darkness of his mind, closing in on him with a terrible certainty.

Grandpa hit the brakes a little too hard, and even the 4-wheel-drive of the Scout couldn't keep it from sliding off to the right to gently slap a bank of ploughed snow. Alan watched his grandfather as he turned and stared at the stranger.

'Listen, mister, I don't know what your game is, but I don't find it very amusin' like you seem to . . . And I don't appreciate the way you've dealt with our hospitality.'

Grandpa glared at the man in the back seat, and Alan could feel the courage burning behind the old man's eyes. Just the sight of it gave Alan the strength to turn and face the stranger.

'Just trying to make conversation,' said the man in a velvety-soft voice. It seemed to Alan that the stranger's voice could change any time he wanted it to, could sound any way at all. The man in the mask was like a ventriloquist or a magician, maybe . . .

'Well, to be truthful with you, mister,' Grandpa was saying. 'I'm kinda tired of your "conversation", so why don't you climb out right here?'

The eyes behind the mask flitted between Grandpa and Alan once, twice. 'I see . . .' said the voice. 'No more silly stuff, eh?'

The stranger leaned forward, putting a gloved hand on the back of Alan's seat. The hand almost touched Alan's parka and he pulled away. He knew he didn't want the stranger touching him. Acid churned in his stomach.

'Very well,' said the dark man. 'I'll be leaving you for now . . . but one last thought, all right?'

'I'd rather not,' said Grandpa, as the man squeezed out of the open passenger's door.

'But you will . . .' Another soft laugh as the stranger stood in the drifted snow alongside the road. The eyes behind the mask darted from Grandpa to Alan and back again. 'You see, it's just a short ride we're all taking . . . and the night is freezing fast.'

Grandpa's eyes widened a bit as the words drifted slowly into the cab, cutting through the swirling, whipping-cold wind. Then he gunned the gas-pedal. 'Goodbye, mister . . .'

The Scout suddenly leaped forward in the snow with such force that Alan didn't have to pull the door closed—it slammed shut from the force of the acceleration.

Looking back, Alan could see the stranger quickly dwindle to nothing more than a black speck on the white wall behind them.

'Of all the people to be helpful to, and I have to pick a danged nut!' Grandpa forced a smile to his face. He looked at Alan and tapped his arm playfully. 'Nothin' to worry about now, boy. He's behind us and gone.'

'Who you figure he was?'

'Oh, just a nut, son. A kook. When you get older you'll realize that there's lots of "funny" people in the world.'

'You think he'll still be out on the road when we go back?'

Grandpa looked at Alan and tried to smile. It was an effort and it didn't look anything at all like a real smile.

'You were afraid of him, weren't you, boy?'

Alan nodded. 'Weren't *you*?'

Grandpa didn't answer for an instant. He certainly *looked* scared. Then: 'Well, kinda, I guess. But I've known about his type. Everybody runs into 'im . . . sooner or later, I guess.'

'Really?' Alan didn't understand what the old man meant.

Grandpa looked ahead. 'Well, here's the store . . .'

After parking, Grandpa ran into the Food-A-Rama for a pound of butter while Alan remained in the cab with the engine running, the heater fan wailing, and the doors locked. Looking out into the swirling snow, Alan could barely pick out single flakes any more. Everything was blending into a furiously thick, white mist. The windows of the Scout were blank sheets of paper, he could see *nothing* beyond the glass.

Suddenly there was a dark shape at the driver's side, and the latch rattled on the door handle. The lock flipped up and Grandpa appeared with a small brown paper bag in his hand. 'Boy, it's blowin' up terrible out here! What a time that woman has to send us out!'

'It looks worse,' said Alan.

'Well, maybe not,' said Grandpa, slipping the vehicle into gear. 'Night's coming on. When it gets darker, the white-out won't be as bad.'

They drove home along Route 28, which would eventually curve down and cross 14A. Alan fidgeted with the heater fan and the cab was finally starting to warm up a little bit. He felt better, but he couldn't get the stranger's voice out of his mind.

'Grandpa, what did that man mean about "a short ride" we're all taking? And about the night freezing fast?'

'I don't rightly know what he meant, Alan. He was a kook,

remember? He probably don't know himself what he meant by it . . .'

'Well, he sure did make it sound creepy, didn't he?'

'Yes, I guess he did,' said Grandpa as he turned the wheel onto a crossing road. 'Here we go, here's 14A. Almost home, boy! I hope your grandmother's got that fireplace hot!'

The Scout trundled along the snowed-up road until they reached a bright orange mailbox that marked the entrance to Grandpa's farm. Alan exhaled slowly, and felt the relief spreading into his bones. He hadn't wanted to say anything, but the white-white of the storm and the seeping cold had been bothering him, making him get a terrible headache, probably from squinting so much.

'*What* in—?' Grandpa eased off the accelerator as he saw the tall, thin figure standing in the snow-filled rut of the driveway.

'It's *him*, Grandpa . . .' said Alan in a whisper.

The dark man stepped aside as the Scout eased up to him. Angrily, Grandpa wound down the window, and let the storm rush into the cab. He shouted past the wind at the stranger. 'You've got a lot of nerve comin' up to my house!'

The eyes behind the ski mask seemed to grow darker, unblinking. 'Didn't have much choice,' said the chameleon-voice.

Grandpa unlocked the door, and stepped out to face the man. 'What do you mean by that?'

Soft laughter cut through the howl of the wind. 'Come now! You *know* who I am . . . and *why* I'm here.'

The words seemed to stop Grandpa in his tracks. Alan watched the old man's face flash suddenly pale. Grandpa nodded. 'Maybe,' he said. 'But I never knew it to be like this . . .'

'There are countless ways,' said the stranger. 'Now excuse me, and step aside . . .'

'What?' Grandpa sounded shocked.

Alan had climbed down from the Scout, standing behind the two men. He could hear naked terror couched in the back of his grandfather's throat, the trembling fear in his voice. Without realizing it, Alan was backing away from the Scout. His head was pounding like a jackhammer.

'Is it the *woman*?' Grandpa was asking in a whisper.

The dark man shook his head.

Grandpa moaned loudly, letting it turn into words. 'No! Not *him*! No, you can't mean it!'

'Aneurysm . . .' said the terribly soft voice behind the mask.

Suddenly Grandpa grabbed the stranger by the shoulder, and spun him around, facing him squarely. 'No!' he shouted, his face twisted and ugly. 'Me! Take me!'

'Can't do it,' said the man.

'Grandpa, what's the matter?!' Alan started to feel dizzy. The pounding in his head had become a raging fire. It hurt so bad he wanted to scream.

'Yes you can!' yelled Grandpa. 'I *know* you can!'

Alan watched as Grandpa reached out and grabbed at the tall thin man's ski mask. It seemed to come apart as he touched it, and fell away from beneath the droopy brimmed hat. For an instant, Alan could see—or at least he *thought* he saw—*nothing* beneath the mask. It was like staring into a night sky and suddenly realizing the *endlessness*, the eternity of it all. To Alan, it was just an eye-blink of time, and then he saw, for another instant, white, angular lines, dark hollows of empty sockets.

But the snow was swirling and whipping, and Grandpa was suddenly wrestling with the man, and the ache in his head was almost blinding him now. Alan screamed as the man wrapped his long thin arms around his grandfather and they seemed to dance briefly around in the snow.

'Run, boy!' screamed Grandpa.

Alan turned towards the house, then looked back and he saw Grandpa collapsing into the snow. The tall, dark man was gone.

'Grandpa!' Alan ran to the old man's side as he lay face up, his glazed eyes staring into the storm.

'Get your grandmother . . . quick,' said the old man. 'It's my heart.'

'Don't die, Grandpa . . . not now!' Alan was frantic and didn't know what to do. He wanted to get help, but didn't want to leave his grandfather in the storm like this.

'No choice in it,' he said. 'A deal's a deal.'

Alan looked at his grandfather, suddenly puzzled. 'What?'

Grandpa winced as new pain lanced his chest. 'Don't matter now . . .' The old man closed his eyes and wheezed out a final breath.

Snowflakes danced across his face, and Alan noticed that his headache, like the dark man, had vanished.

Night in Paris

Patrice Chaplin

FOR Christmas 1950 when Lucy was eleven, Aunt Ethel sent her a bottle of perfume. It was called 'Night in Paris' and was packaged in a blue box with an Eiffel Tower and a half moon on the front. It was Lucy's first glamorous present and she was so thrilled she wanted to keep it forever. That was her first mistake. Her second was standing it on the dressing-table next to the glossy postcard photographs of her film star favourites, Lauren Bacall and Robert Taylor. Since she was six she'd wanted to be a film star. The 'Night in Paris' perfume seemed to help that along. Enclosed in the wrapping paper was a note from Aunt Ethel. 'To My Darling Dearest Little God Daughter. Auntie's so proud you've won a place at Grammar School.'

In those days Lucy had a shilling a week pocket money invariably spent in Woolworth's at the make-up counter. She could buy a small bottle of Eau de Cologne for tenpence or a mirror and powder puff in a plastic case for fourpence. Colourless nail varnish was a shilling, face-powder ninepence. The 'Night in Paris' perfume adorned Woolworth's counter in many sizes. The deluxe bottle cost two and nine. After the glamour shopping she went to Saturday afternoon pictures at the Odeon. She'd earned the one and three ticket money washing up in the High Street café.

That Christmas, 1950, her mother received a stiff mauve folder with a satin bow on the front. The writing paper and envelopes inside smelt of lavender. Lucy had seen the present in Woolworth's at three and six. Her mother opened the folder. 'Good, Ethel hasn't written in it. I can give it to your Auntie Vi. I don't need posh stuff like this.' And she put it away in the dressing-table.

Auntie Vi arrived Boxing Day and brought not only a present but her daughter, young Violet, also bearing a gift. Lucy's mother rushed into the bedroom and got out the writing paper. She turned the mauve folder over to scribble a greeting on the back. The price, five shillings, was inked boldly in the corner.

'But that isn't right,' said Lucy. 'It's only three and six. I've seen it in Woolworth's.'

'They don't ink in the prices either. That's your Aunt Ethel. Swank as usual. We'll have to give young Violet something.' Her mother looked around wildly. 'Give her the scent. Come on. You can always get some more.'

Lucy was appalled. 'But it's too good even to use.'

'All the better. Not been touched. They can see that. Come on. Hurry up. They've come all the way from Gosport.' Lucy's mother always got her way in those days.

Reluctantly Lucy wrote on the back of the box: 'To my Cousin Violet with love, Christmas 50.' In exchange she received a doll's hood.

In 1952 Lucy again received a bottle of 'Night in Paris' perfume for Christmas. This time it came from the Reverend Maude and his wife who lived in Weymouth. Lucy wouldn't have thought twice about it if she hadn't seen, faintly scratched on the box, 'Cousin Violet . . . 50.'

Her mother said for all the Reverend Maude's snobbery he was a cheapskate. 'But how did they get my present that I passed on to Cousin Violet?'

'Your cousin was made to send it on to the Reverend's wife, that's why. Your Aunty Vi wouldn't let her daughter use that muck. You know the sort who use that.'

That year Lucy had started wearing 'Californian Poppy' perfume, Woolworth's one and six a bottle, so she decided to put the present in her drawer until the other was finished. When she came to use it, however, it had gone. Her mother had sent it to Aunt Ethel for her birthday. 'But she sent it to me originally!' Lucy was outraged.

'She won't know. She ought to be glad to get anything. Mutton dressed as lamb.'

The photographs of Lauren Bacall and Robert Taylor had gone too. So had most of Lucy's film star collection which she kept in a shoebox in the wardrobe. She hadn't noticed because she was so passionately in love with Mario Lanza after seeing him in *Because You're Mine* and *The Great Caruso* that only pictures of him adorned her room.

Her mother admitted she'd given them to Cousin Violet. 'You don't want those old photographs. She's only a kid. Gives her something to look at.'

Lucy realized her mother, along with Aunt Ethel, had no respect for possessions. The film stars had taken years to collect. She'd written to the stars care of the studios and usually got a signed glossy photograph in reply. Vera Ellen, Cornel Wilde, Lana Turner, Ava Gardner, Humphrey Bogart, Phyllis Calvert—they'd given dreams and brightened up her dreary schooldays in the suburbs. She tried to explain that to her mother.

'Give all that up. You're not a child. You're nearly fourteen.'

'But I want to be one of them.'

'Make believe. You've got to get on with the real world.' Her mother wanted Lucy to become a private secretary. That's where the status was. Film stars played no part in that job.

The next Christmas Lucy received a stiff mauve folder of writing paper from Aunt Ethel. Written inside in blue ink was, 'To my Darling Little God Daughter with heaps of love and affection for Christmas 1953. P.S. Only a little gift darling but you can write more letters to your Auntie.' A gummed label on the top right hand corner marked the price. Twelve and sixpence. Lucy tore it off and underneath was inked five shillings, the price Aunt Ethel had originally marked it up to when she'd sent it, all festive and indisputably new, to Lucy's mother in 1950. Lucy sniffed the folder. The lavender smell had gone. The mauve silk bow was flattened and frayed and Aunt Ethel had disguised its age by sewing on a cloth rose.

'What a cheek!'

'Doesn't matter.' Lucy's mother grabbed the folder. 'We'll try and scratch the price out and send it to the Reverend Maude and his wife.'

'But Ethel's written in it!'

'They'll never know. They're half blind. I'll stick a label over the message. Ethel's a nuisance, writing all over the presents like that.'

Lucy got an expensive gift from the Reverend Maude and his wife. A bottle of Coty 'Chypre' fragrance in an untampered box. Lucy hadn't seen it in Woolworth's—it was out of that price range.

'I wonder who gave her that,' said Lucy's mother. 'She can't stand scent, old Maude's wife. That's why you've got it.'

By Easter the Mario Lanza pictures were down and the bedroom wall was bare. Lucy had a crush on her gym mistress and was longing to give her a token of the passion. The Chypre fragrance was undeniably right. A memorable gift of love. Lucy began the accompanying note and her mother picked up the bottle.

'Where's this going?'

'To my teacher. It's her birthday.'

'Rubbish. These are Christmas presents. You don't touch these.'

'But it's valuable.'

'All the better. Do for Aunt Ethel. She's come up in the world. She's going to manage a hotel in the Isle of Wight.'

'But it's mine.'

Her mother kept her hands on the Chypre. 'But they're sent out at Christmas. You don't use them.'

Lucy longed for revenge. What better than an incorruptible present, the transitory kind. Next Christmas she'd send out a batch of live things that died. Plants. Unheard of in the Christmas chain. She even considered perishable things like home-made cakes covered in hundreds and thousands or blancmange packed in ice.

Lucy loved Christmas. She loved cards and carols, crackers, coal fires, party games. From the end of November each year she went carol singing with her friends and they saved the money to buy presents. Lucy enjoyed wrapping them, decorating the packages with holly and tinsel. The professional presents upset her.

In the late forties a special present had gone into circulation but it didn't reach Lucy until the mid-fifties. A small tin of Snowfire vanishing cream, Woolworth's one and three. It was considered a suitable professional gift because the tin couldn't be marked and by lifting the lid it was obvious it hadn't been used. It was passed on to Aunt Ethel for Christmas '55 and she recognized its pedigree. In the same wrapping it was despatched to little Beryl in Folkestone. Aged ten, the girl was delighted. Her mother took it away. 'Whatever is Ethel thinking about? You don't want to put muck on your face at your age.' She rewrapped it immediately and sent it to Lucy. 'A late present for my pretty niece.' If she put that old cream on her face, Lucy reflected, the adjective might cease to apply. It lay in the darkness of her dressing-table for years. Before they moved in 1959 her mother removed it from the box of jumble. 'Wait a minute. This stuff's never been used. It might come in for someone.' Aunt Ethel got it with a tin of tea the following Christmas.

Lucy had rejected the secretarial path. After school she'd worked in the local rep as ASM and made her way up to juvenile lead. She was glamorous and earned extra money fashion modelling in London. She no longer shopped at Woolworth's. In 1960, after she'd failed to get a small part in a West End pantomime, she was obliged to visit Aunt Ethel. The Reverend Maude and his wife were also staying. It was a subdued Christmas but she did get one laugh. When Aunt Ethel opened her presents Vi and young Violet had sent a folder of writing paper and a slightly battered box of 'Night in Paris' perfume. Fourteen and six was inked outrageously on the side. Aunt Ethel grimaced but her voice was bright. 'How nice. They don't always have such taste about present giving.'

Both the satin bow and cloth rose had gone from the folder and the gluey scar was covered by a handmade paper doll that leaned forward when the folder was opened.

'How original,' said Lucy mischievously.

Aunt Ethel's mouth tightened. 'Yes. Young Violet was always good at craft.' The Reverend Maude's wife received the Snowfire vanishing cream. It was the first time she'd got that. The Coty 'Chypre' fragrance had gone into hiding.

Lucy gave them a completely innocent present. It could not be

corrupted. She laid the plucked goose onto the table. They pretended to be grateful but they were very disappointed. Didn't Lucy know the meaning of Christmas?

All three long-term festive missiles ended up in Aunt Ethel's care. She let them freshen up in her dressing-table pungent with the smell of old Christmas soaps and thirties lavender bags for two years. Then she took the 'Night in Paris' scent and removed it from its box. She wrapped it in an Irish linen handkerchief (Christmas '37) and sent it to young Beryl in Folkestone. She removed the handmade doll from the stationery folder, stuck a Christmas label over the glue mark and wrote right across the front of the folder in indelible red pen, 'Happy Christmas'. In a moment of spite she added '1967'. She gave it to the Reverend Maude. He was ninety-four and had a short memory. So did she it seemed in '68 because she gave the Snowfire cream to Lucy for her birthday. She arrived unannounced in the dressing-room of the West End theatre while Lucy was on stage and left a note. 'Just dropped in on a flying visit with little gifts for my clever God daughter.' Lucy kept the tin in the dressing-room and the other actresses were intrigued by its age, its nostalgia.

The second 'little present' was the film star collection which Lucy had so loved as a child. 'I thought you might like these. I got them for you especially. They're very valuable, darling.'

More than Aunt Ethel could know. How she'd got them from

Cousin Violet and what circuitous route they'd travelled, Lucy could not guess.

There was an outbreak of the professional presents in 1971 but by then Lucy was in Hollywood. 'Night in Paris' was still going strong. It travelled around as part of a Boots toilet selection. The writing paper had had to come off the circuit in '68. Lucy's mother had received it from the Reverend Maude and the seven of sixty-seven had been changed to a spidery eight. Lucy's mother was licked. She kept it in the dressing-table until she could think of something to do with it.

Aunt Ethel wrote to Hollywood where Lucy was playing small parts. 'We so missed you at Christmas but if you do get back to England there's a welcome home present waiting at your mother's. It may come in useful for your busy career. We're so proud of you.'

When Lucy finally returned in 1976 after her mother's death, she found the little gift in the sideboard. She lifted off the soft blue crêpe paper and on a nest of green nineteen-fifties taffeta lay the bottle of 'Night in Paris'. She hadn't seen it for years. Its smell took her back to her school days, Mario Lanza, the crush on the gym teacher, carol singing. It also reminded her of the Christmases of the war. Waking up early in the cold with the blackout still up and under the dim torch light unwrapping a small packet of perfumed crayons, six colours and a drawing book, some nuts wrapped in silver paper, a packet of Cadbury's chocolate with purple wrapping, a monkey up a stick, an apple, an orange. One year there was the magic of a kaleidoscope. She remembered these as being the happy Christmases.

She took the folder of writing paper from her mother's table, smelling of mothballs. She tore off the two strips of satin ribbon and took out a yellowing envelope and sheet of paper. She wrote,

'Thank you, Auntie Ethel, for all the Christmases.'

Swiftbuck's Christmas Carol

Francis Beckett

O H, yes,' said the Ghost of Christmas Past, lying back in his big armchair and resting his stockinged feet on the fender so they would feel the heat of the roaring log fire. 'We've seen a few scoundrels in our time, haven't we, Porky?'

He always called her Porky, because her real name was so long-winded that he could never hold a conversation with her if he used it. I mean, imagine having to say 'Isn't that right, Ghost of Christmas Yet to Come' every time you talked to someone. And it amused him to call her Porky, because she was excessively thin.

'We have, Maximilian,' said the Ghost of Christmas Yet to Come from her perch on the radiator the other side of the room. She didn't like wood fires. Smelly, dirty things, she thought, and why put up with them when you could have central heating. 'That Ebenezer Scrooge who everyone talks about, he wasn't the worst of them, not by any means.'

'Not by any means at all,' said Maximilian, stifling a yawn and reaching out for his comforting glass of mulled wine. 'At least Scrooge knew what a miserable old scrooge he was. Now, you take that fellow we looked at last year. What was his name again?'

'Swiftbuck,' said Porky. 'Swiftbuck the internet millionaire. Now, he thought he was generous, didn't he? Come Christmas time, he'd throw a fine party for all the people who worked for him. But I saw through that.'

'What do you mean, you saw through that? I saw through it first.'

'Of course you saw through it first, because you went there first, you stupid old ghost. You always do. That's why you're the Ghost of Christmas Past. But you were taken in by him at first. I saw through him the moment I saw him.'

'Wasn't my fault.' Maximilian looked moodily into the fire. 'There he was. Come on, lads and lasses, he'd say, come to the best hotel, eat the best food, drink champagne, it's all on Swiftbuck. I thought: he's no Scrooge, old Swiftbuck. How was I to know? I found him out in the end, though. Oh, yes. He couldn't fool me for long. I'm too long in the tooth for that.'

And as he watched the flames dancing over the red hot logs in the fire, he seemed to see the face of Swiftbuck, with that open, generous, kindly smile that he remembered so well, just as it was that moment when Maximilian at last realized the terrible truth.

It was two weeks before Christmas. Swiftbuck always used to say: 'For my people, Christmas starts two weeks early, because my people deserve a good time.' And indeed, it was a fine party.

Maximilian shouldn't really have been at that party at all. He had already certified Swiftbuck as a Grade A Generous Chap, and he should have been out that Christmas looking for stingy scoundrels. But he liked Swiftbuck's parties. He liked the cheerfulness on all the faces, the laughter and the jokes, the music. He liked the way Swiftbuck provided the best of everything. The wine flowed freely, and an unseen ghost could get his hands on a crafty glass or two of fine champagne without anyone noticing. Most of all, he liked watching Swiftbuck himself, moving smoothly among his guests—a kind word here, a shared joke there, always a wide, inclusive smile.

Maximilian was enjoying himself so much that he almost missed the moment when it happened. He had just noticed an unattended bottle of champagne, and was making his silent and invisible way across the room, when his eye caught two rather pretty young women whom he thought he recognized from Swiftbuck's office.

'What's happened to Rosie?' said one of the young women. 'She's not here. And she wasn't in the office yesterday.'

'Didn't you hear?' And the other woman made a slitting sign across her throat.

Maximilian stopped in his tracks. He'd wondered vaguely himself why Rosie wasn't there—cheerful, friendly Rosie, always willing to help anyone in trouble, the person in Swiftbuck's office whom everyone else took their troubles to.

'Swiftbuck fired her?' The young woman could hardly believe it. 'Poor Rosie, didn't she have troubles enough already? Why did he do a thing like that?'

'Wasn't meeting her sales targets. That's what I hear.'

'What's she going to do? What about the children? How could he do that—to Rosie of all people?' But her friend suddenly put her finger to her mouth, for she had seen, over the other's shoulder, Swiftbuck coming across to them, his warm, tender smile carefully glued onto his face.

'Well, after that, I said to myself, no time to waste, Maximilian, old son.' The Ghost of Christmas Past reached across to a saucepan resting on a grille over the open fire, picked up a huge ladle, and poured himself another glass of the steaming purple wine.

'I bet you were on to that like a flash,' said the Ghost of Christmas Yet to Come sarcastically.

'I'm not as young as I look, Porky old dear, but I got there. One night, textbook operation it was, crept in through the window—damn new-fangled houses don't have chimneys, y'know. Woke old Swiftbuck. Swiftbuck, I said, come you along o' me. Showed him what his own Christmases were like as a child.

'They were pretty good, you know. House all filled with presents and pudding. His parents, you know, they weren't rich, but they weren't poor either, and they thought the world of him, nothing was too good for their son. Saw a tear in his eye as he watched his mother filling his Christmas stocking. Thought to myself, Maximilian old chum, you and your ghostly pals are about to score again. Just show him what Rosie's Christmas is like now he's fired her, and the job's done.

'Well, of course, for that I needed the Ghost of Christmas Present, and you know what she's like.'

'Away on one of her experiments, I suppose,' sniffed Porky. 'She's never there when you want her.'

'Ghost of Christmas Present indeed,' huffed Maximilian. 'Ghost of Christmas Absent, more like. I was getting worried, thought Christmas would be over and done with before she turned up. I was sending spirits all over the globe with messages for her.'

'Didn't go looking for her yourself, I suppose?' Porky sounded a little as though she thought he ought to have done.

'Someone had to stay here in case she turned up.'

'Right here, by the fire, with the mulled wine?'

'That's it,' said Maximilian cheerfully, and if he noticed the irony in his fellow ghost's tone of voice, he wasn't letting on. 'And I was right. Morning of Christmas Eve, it was, I was sitting here, in this very chair, thinking, we won't be able to do the job in time, when in she came. And off we went.'

'We? Did you go along too?'

'I did,' said Maximilian. 'Rosie, you see, had sent her children to stay with a friend. There she was, all alone. So I went along to look after Swiftbuck, make sure he heard everything they said, while the Ghost of Christmas Present talked to her.'

'Talked to her! You mean she materialized?'

'Had to, old sausage. Nothing for Swiftbuck to hear if Rosie didn't have someone to talk to.'

'But it's against all the rules. Hasn't she read Merlin on Ghosting?'

'Used to be done a lot in the old days, materializing,' said Maximilian. 'Before Charles Dickens came along and wrote about us, and we had to start being careful and discreet. I may be old fashioned . . .'

'Oh, come on! Dickens dragged us into the second half of the millennium.'

'Maybe, maybe. Anyway, sometimes you have to break the rules, and this was one of them. She couldn't have done the job otherwise.'

The Ghost of Christmas Present had appeared to Rosie as a woman called Crumbly—which as it happens was the name her fellow ghosts used for her. She befriended Rosie in the supermarket, and accepted her invitation to come home for a cup of tea.

They sat in Rosie's kitchen on upturned boxes, sipping their tea out of chipped mugs and looking at the suitcases, wooden packing cases, and furniture with labels on, which lined the walls. Maximilian and Swiftbuck were an invisible audience.

'Yes,' said Rosie. 'I'll be out of here tomorrow. No point in keeping on the house when I know I won't be able to pay the mortgage next month.'

'You've sent the children away?' said Crumbly.

'This has been their home all their lives,' said Rosie. 'Their father died in this house. I haven't told them we're losing it. If I can find another job somewhere, I'll be able to rent a small flat, then they can come and live with me again.'

'How did it happen?' said Crumbly. 'Why did Swiftbuck do this to you?'

'Oh.' Rosie held her teacup in both hands underneath her chin and seemed to be looking at the far wall. 'Swiftbuck, you have to hand it to him, was one of the first people to work out that if you sold things to people over the internet, you could employ far fewer people, you could cut your costs, and so you could make much bigger profits.

'I went to work for Swiftbuck nearly two years ago. That doesn't sound long, but it's a long, long time in the internet business. People are in and out of that office in weeks. But I stayed, because Swiftbuck said he needed me there. I was the calm, sensible one. I don't know why,' she said with a long sigh, 'but I always seem to be the calm, sensible one.

'When anything went wrong in the office, they turned to me. When the systems didn't work, I put them right. When one of the girls had boyfriend trouble, I sorted it out. I kept everything going efficiently, looked after everyone and made them feel at home, so Swiftbuck could get on with expanding the business.

'It's not hard really,' she added thoughtfully. 'When you've looked after two children, looking after twenty people in an office is easy.

Anyway,' she said, 'I don't have any qualifications. I was lucky to have the job.

'Then, just about the start of November, he came to me. I just had the feeling there was something wrong. His smile was a bit wider than usual, he sounded—I don't know—as though he really, really cared about me, and that bothered me, I don't know why.

'He said: "You're not contributing to the bottom line, Rosie, my love." And he said it with such a kind smile on his face, the sort of smile that seemed to say: I'm going to look after you. Then he said: "Of course everyone loves you, but you're not bringing any money into the company. Anyone who works here has to contribute to profits. That's the way a business works." And he made me give up the job I loved and join the sales team. Ring people up, get them to log on to our website, tell them how safe it is to give us their credit card details, that sort of thing.

'But what I didn't know was that he logged every call, and got the computer to show him who was turning their calls into business and who wasn't. And of course, I wasn't. I wasn't any good at that sort of thing. So the day before the party, Swiftbuck fired me.

'Then he said: "Best you don't come to the party tomorrow, my love." He said it in his kindest tone of voice, and I was sure he was only thinking of me. "No point in making yourself unhappy and everybody else uncomfortable." And do you know, that upset me more than anything.'

She paused, and Crumbly said: 'I know what you mean. When something really bad happens, we often get most upset about the bits that don't really matter.'

'I made all the arrangements for that party,' said Rosie. 'I booked the hotel, chose the music, ordered the wine and the food, and I was looking forward to it. It was the idea that I wouldn't be at the party that finally made me cry.

'But then I thought: this is no good. I washed my face, stood up straight, and marched into Swiftbuck's office. Told him he couldn't fire me just like that. I had rights. If he wanted to get rid of me, he had to pay me off. That's what the law says.'

'That's the spirit,' said Crumbly.

'But he'd been clever, you see. When he'd taken me away from my old job, he'd asked me to sign a new contract. And that said that he could fire me whenever he liked. And he said: "That's the real world, I'm afraid, Rosie, my love," and he flashed me that huge, reassuring smile.'

Crumbly said: 'I bet it's made a mess of the children's Christmas.'

'Oh, Crumbly, you've no idea.' Rosie's eyes filled with tears. 'I'd promised my fourteen year old, Daniel, a Playstation, and Jenny— she's eleven—all she wanted was some books—and now they can't have anything. They can't even live in their own house any more. I haven't told them about the house yet, they were so disappointed about the presents that I couldn't bring myself to tell them we were losing the house too. I don't know how I'll ever bring myself to tell them.'

'Sounds quite a show you two ghosts were able to lay on for old Swiftbuck,' said Porky coldly. 'Shame it didn't work. After you'd shown him all that, you still had to come and get me out of bed that night.'

'We took Swiftbuck home,' said Maximilian, 'and we waited for that moment, you know, when they burst into tears, say they'll be reformed characters forever, go about doing good deeds—you know, you've seen it, gives you a sort of glow inside every time. And we didn't see it. He went straight back to sleep. Well, of course, we thought, don't like to bother the Ghost of Christmas Yet to Come, Christmas Eve and all that, but . . .'

'But you did,' said the Ghost of Christmas Yet to Come. '"Come on, Porky", you said, "we've made a mess of it again, the Ghost of Christmas Present and I, and we need you to sort it out."'

'That's not what we said.'

'It's what you meant.'

So the Ghost of Christmas Yet to Come took Swiftbuck to his own funeral, at Christmas time forty years after he had fired Rosie. He was able to see the dark clothes of the mourners, to hear the speech about what a fine chap he had been. Such a great public benefactor, apparently, that the queen had given him a knighthood. That really tickled him, everyone talking about Sir Darren Swiftbuck.

But then Porky took him inside the hearts of these mourners, and let him see what they were really thinking. And, of course, secretly they were all glad he was dead. Such a miserable, selfish, conniving, mean, and greedy man, they thought.

'And that did the trick,' said Porky, in that slightly self-satisfied tone which the Ghost of Christmas Past always found rather irritating. 'He went straight round and gave Rosie her job back.'

Suddenly there was a deafening roaring sound in the room, like a great hurricane. The calm stillness was broken abruptly, as the wind whistled round the walls, blowing out the fire and throwing the Ghost of Christmas Past out of his chair onto the floor. His mulled wine formed into waves in its saucepan, like a mighty ocean in a hurricane. The lights flickered, and even Porky had to get up from her perch on the radiator and wedge herself in a corner.

Slowly, a figure started to appear in the middle of the floor—a tall, dignified figure, with flowing white robes, long, dark hair, and an expression of fury on its face. The noise became quieter, the wind dropped, and Maximilian looked up from the floor.

'For heaven's sake, Crumbly, why can't you just shimmer through the walls like a normal ghost?' he said irritably.

'No time,' said the Ghost of Christmas Present breathlessly. 'It's an emergency.'

'It's always an emergency with you,' said Porky. 'You just like being dramatic.'

'It's Swiftbuck.'

'Swiftbuck?' said Maximilian.

'We were just recalling,' said Porky, 'how I cracked that one after you and Maximilian here failed.'

'That's what you think,' said the Ghost of Christmas Present, and if there was a hint of triumph in her voice, the other two pretended not to notice. 'You know how I like to check on them, one year afterwards. Right back to his old ways, he is. Fired Rosie again this Christmas, and says he won't change his mind this time. Well, of course, I went

into his bedroom and woke him up. He was a bit alarmed at first, of course . . .'

'I bet he was,' said Maximilian, who had just succeeded in getting the fire going again. 'But just frightening people with theatrical tricks doesn't do any good at all in the long run.'

Crumbly ignored him.

'But when he recognized me,' she said, 'do you know, he smiled. And this is what he said: "Listen up, Ghost of Christmas Present . . . "'

'Is "listen up" some kind of twenty-first century Americanism?' asked Maximilian grumpily.

'"Listen up, Ghost of Christmas Present. There's no percentage in being a nice person. There might have been when you ghosts were frightening people years ago, but the world's moved on. Now, there's only one thing that matters, and that's success. And there's only one person to look after, and that's yourself. Wake up and smell the coffee."'

'Poor Rosie,' said Maximilian.

'Don't worry about Rosie,' said Crumbly. 'Swiftbuck doesn't know, but she thought this might happen. She learned her lesson last year. This time, she's prepared for it. She did some evening classes, and she's got another job. It's Swiftbuck I'm worried about. We never used to fail like this. I just have the feeling that things are getting tougher now than they've ever been.'

There was a long silence, broken at last by the Ghost of Christmas Yet to Come. The other two noticed an unusual intensity in her voice. She didn't sound like the slightly waspish ghost they'd always known.

'What they've done in the twenty-first century,' she said, 'is something they never thought of in old Charles Dickens's day. They've made greed and selfishness into virtues. And until we train them out of that, I'm afraid we're going to have more failures like Swiftbuck.'

'Last time I heard you speaking in that tone of voice,' said Maximilian, 'there was no peace for months. Do this, go there, talk to Scrooge.'

'It's that and more,' said Porky grimly. 'This is going to be harder than anything we've ever done.'

Her two companions digested this for a while. At last the Ghost of Christmas Past heaved a long sigh.

'Might as well get ready for work,' he said, and fortified the remaining mulled wine with a drop of brandy.

Josef's Carol
Alison Prince

JAMIE White walked home from school in the blustery November afternoon, up the steep cart track that led to his house. Far below him on his left, visible between the tossing branches of the trees, the sea was white-patched with breaking waves. A storm was gathering, but Jamie paid no attention to it. He was more interested in talking to Josef. 'Mum and Dad are still wanting to sell the house,' he said. 'They keep on about moving down to the town so as to be nearer to the High School when I start next year. But that's just an excuse.'

'Then what is the real reason?' asked Josef. He sounded almost amused, as if he already knew what was going on.

'I think it's because they don't like me talking to you,' said Jamie resentfully. 'And Miss Mayhew's just as bad. Look at all the fuss she made about you being in the classroom.'

Josef sighed. 'They are so stupid,' he said. 'I am always very quiet at school. And it is months since I have been in your house.'

'I know,' Jamie agreed. 'But they don't seem to like the idea that you're about at all. It's so unreasonable.'

There was a silence. Jamie plodded on up the track with his shoulders hunched against the wind, and wondered if his friend had gone into a sulk. But when Josef spoke again, his voice was apologetic and a little embarrassed. 'It doesn't really matter what they think,' he said. 'You see, I have to go away, too. I've been meaning to tell you.'

'But why?' asked Jamie, astonished. Josef had always been here, ever since the day when Jamie had first found him, up the hill in the old building they called 'the cathedral'.

Josef hesitated. 'It's not easy to explain,' he said. 'I was—left here. It happens sometimes. When people have to go away from a place they love, a part of them gets left behind. But, in the end, they will come back, to be complete again.'

'What are you *talking* about?' Jamie demanded irritably.

'I can't tell you any more now,' said Josef. 'Your mother is waiting.'

Jamie rounded the last sharp bend in the track and glanced up, to see that what his friend had said was true. His mother stood by the gate with folded arms, her long cardigan wrapped tightly round her against the attacking wind. He was touched to see her standing there, and yet her presence at this moment was thoroughly inconvenient. 'I'll come up later,' he muttered to Josef. 'I want to know what you mean.'

There was no answer, but the cloud-streaked sky above the hill's edge seemed a little more ominous in Josef's absence.

'Hello!' Jamie's mother called to him. 'What a day! We're in for a real storm!'

'Looks like it,' he agreed. He wondered what she had to tell him. She would not come to the gate in weather like this unless there was a bit of news to impart.

'Some people are here to look at the house,' she said. 'A woman with an old chap who doesn't speak. I think he's her uncle or something. But she seems to like the place. She's quite keen to buy it.'

Jamie understood the message. He had to be quiet and polite, and his bedroom would have been tidied up. He scowled. 'I don't want us to move away,' he said again. 'I like it here.'

'Once you get used to the new house, you'll love it,' his mother assured him, trying to sound patient. 'You'll make a lot of new friends at the High School and they'll be able to come in for tea—not like here, where they've such a long walk back again, and in the dark if it's winter time. You've got used to being on your own, Jamie. You don't realize how unnatural it is.'

They walked up the path to the house, which stood backed into the hill like a sheltering sheep. Jamie did not pursue the argument. The word 'unnatural' was a warning sign. Once it had been spoken, they were on the slippery slope to a tirade about daydreams and unhealthy imaginings and the general undesirability of a friend whom nobody could see.

Jamie hung up his anorak in the hall and glanced without curiosity into the little-used sitting-room as his mother opened its door and went in with a cheerful cry of, 'More tea for anyone?' He caught a glimpse of a woman in a fur coat and a solidly-built man with thick white hair. They were intruders, he thought. The very smell of them was alien, as if they were big lumps of machinery rather than humans.

'Jamie, come and meet Mrs Pringle,' his mother instructed.

Jamie scowled at the carpet as he was introduced to the visitors. He could feel the woman's smile like a kind of stickiness on his skin and clothes. Looking up reluctantly from under his eyebrows, he encountered the gaze of the white-haired man, who sat on a wooden chair by the window with his hands in his lap. At least, Jamie thought, he was not smiling.

Mrs Pringle intercepted Jamie's glance and said, 'Ah. I hope you won't think him rude, dear, but my uncle doesn't speak. It's what grown-ups call a nervous disorder.' She smiled again, patronizingly, and Jamie felt affronted. Did she think he was stupid? He looked with more interest at the silent man, whose blue eyes stared back dispassionately, registering the presence of Jamie quite neutrally, as if the boy was a continuation of the pattern of the wallpaper.

Mrs Pringle leaned towards Jamie's mother confidentially. 'They think it's because of the background,' she whispered. 'He escaped with his parents from Russia, you see, at the time of the Revolution, and came here, to Scotland.'

Jamie's mother bristled and said, 'I can't see what that's got to do with it.' Jamie felt a flicker of hope. If they were going to quarrel about politics, perhaps the woman would decide against buying the house and go back to London. Evidently the same thought occurred to his mother, because she said quickly, 'But we won't argue about that.'

'No, indeed,' Mrs Pringle agreed. After a pause, she went on, 'I feel that Uncle Joe might benefit from a move up here.' With a sideways glance at the white-haired man, she added, 'He's been in institutions for most of his life, you see, but when he was finally discharged, we agreed to give him a home. Then my husband died.' She gave a helpless shrug. 'So here I am, trying to decide where to live. I thought I might try Scotland. Joe was happy here as a child, or so my husband used to say. He loved it, apparently.'

'Loved this house?' Jamie enquired suddenly.

'I don't know which *house* it was,' said Mrs Pringle with a trace of impatience. 'But they lived somewhere around here.' And she began a long account of how the refugees had made their way across Europe to find their Scottish relatives.

Jamie was not listening. When he had asked his question, the old man's blue eyes had met his own with sharp interest, and he had given a slow, almost imperceptible nod. This *was* the house. Jamie felt his heart beating very fast. Something extraordinary was happening, and it was connected with Josef.

'In the end, they will come back,' he had said. 'To be complete again.' And the old man had come back. Jamie knew he must go and tell Josef. He turned to the door, and saw the old man half-rise from his chair as he did so.

'I expect he wants the loo,' said Mrs Pringle with a sigh. 'Could you possibly—'

'Yes, of course,' said Jamie's mother. 'It's this way.'

Jamie had already escaped. Grabbing his anorak, he let himself out of the back door. He ran up the steps of the garden and through the gate in the back fence, out on to the wind-battered hill. 'Josef!' he called urgently, 'I've got something to tell you!' But the ragged sky brought no answer, and Jamie's words were blown back in his face by the tearing wind. He charged up the hill, following the path which his own feet had worn, a narrow smoothness between the angled-over brown stems of last year's bracken. He reached the forest's edge, where the wind roared with a sound like the sea through the tree tops, and skirted along by the close-planted spruces until he came to the burn.

Here he turned downhill a little way, making for the place where a group of smooth red stones stuck up out of the fast-running water. Jumping from stone to stone, he crossed over and scrambled up the far bank, pushing through the overhanging bushes.

The ruined building was so moss-covered that it hardly looked like a man-made structure at all. It stood on a shelf of flattish ground between the burn and the rocky face of the hill's steeper side, overshadowed by ancient larches and pines, and half-hidden by a vast walnut tree whose branches made a canopy over the crumbling roof. Ferns sprouted from the thick walls in green profusion.

Jamie's eyes were watering from his battle against the wind, and he made his way gratefully towards the shelter of the ruined building. Inside it, he could hear Josef singing, as he had done on that first day, when Jamie had come up the hill exploring, while his parents were still busy unpacking the furniture from the removal van. Now, Josef's voice rose and fell in the yearning melody of that same song. Jamie had come to know it well, joining in the foreign words although he did not understand their meaning. Josef had told him that the song was a carol, about a candle burning in the night before Christmas, and about the singer who kept watch.

Forgetting the urgency of his message, Jamie stood in the doorway and listened, feeling the hair on the back of his neck creep a little in the familiar shiver of something between delight and tears. Josef sang on in his clear alto voice, and Jamie suddenly knew that this was a moment he would never forget. He was acutely aware of the sourness in his throat from the long run up the hill, the pulsing warmth of his feet in their thick socks, and the tingle of painful ecstasy which the music aroused in him. This would be with him for ever.

The carol ended.

Jamie blinked in the dim light which filtered in through the ivy-hung windows and the holes in the roof. The stone floor of the building was higher at one end than the other, with a step between the two levels, and he made his way to this step and sat down. Even after all these years, coming into this place gave him the feeling that he had to collect his thoughts and steady his actions, as if he was entering a church. With a kind of mockery, he had thought of it as 'the cathedral'—and yet it was the grandiose title he mocked, and not the building itself, for even in dereliction, it had a serenity which disarmed all derision.

Then he remembered what he had meant to say. 'Some people have come to the house,' he told Josef. 'An old man who doesn't talk, and a woman called Mrs Pringle. But the old man used to live here, and I wondered if that's what you meant. He's come back.'

There was a pause before Josef answered, and then his voice came from a little distance away, as if he stood at the empty doorway and looked out. 'Yes,' he said. 'That is what I meant.'

'What's going to happen?' asked Jamie fearfully. Again there was no reply for several seconds, and he got up and went to join Josef, folding his arms against the buffeting wind as his mother had done when she stood by the gate with her skirt blowing sideways.

'You have been a good friend,' said Josef, not answering the question. 'I shall be sorry to leave you.'

'Then why go?' demanded Jamie. 'You like it here, don't you? You love this place. So why can't you stay?'

'I have no choice,' said Josef. Absently, he added, 'And perhaps it will be good . . . to be a whole person again.'

Jamie did not know what to say. He felt angry and deprived.

Josef made another effort. 'You know how music makes you feel?' he said. 'As if there is some great struggling thing inside you?'

'Yes,' said Jamie.

'That thing is alive for ever,' Josef told him. 'It is part of the everlasting light. Everything else just comes and goes.'

Jamie grappled with this idea for some moments, then gave up. 'I don't know what you're talking about,' he said.

With one of his sudden changes of mood, Josef burst into a shout of laughter. 'You are wonderful, Jamie!' he declared. 'You never pretend. That's why I love you.'

His laughter was still ringing through the lichened walls of the cathedral when Jamie heard the rhythmic cracking of dry twigs. Somebody was coming through the bushes.

He knew who it would be. Josef's laughter died away. When the man emerged into the clearing, he looked bigger than he had done in the sitting room, solid and thick-necked, with his shock of white hair blown upwards by the wind, like a ragged halo. Jamie watched him, and said nothing.

The man came to a halt. His face was red with the effort of climbing the hill, but his eyes rested on Jamie with clear recognition. His lips moved experimentally, and when the words came they were croaky and shapeless. 'I—was—here,' he said.

Jamie knew he was hearing the first sentence the man had spoken for many years, and the knowledge made him strangely aware of the sound of his own voice as he answered. 'Yes,' he said. 'I know you were.' He felt numb with the dread of something he did not understand. In the forest above them, the wind raged through the trees.

The daylight was fading. The first drops of rain stung Jamie's face, and the wind began a new, high-pitched whistling sound that frightened him. He knew he should not be up here in this weather. From the hillside where the slope was too steep for forestry, he could hear the sharp reports as branches broke from old trees. 'We shouldn't stay here,' he said to the white-haired man. 'It's not safe.'

'Safe,' repeated the man musingly. 'What is safe?' And for a moment, Jamie thought it was Josef's voice which spoke the halting words. It was the kind of thing he so often said.

The white-haired man moved towards the ruined building, and his face softened into a smile. 'I was—happy,' he said. 'Here.' He reached the doorway and paused, just as Jamie always did. Then he went in. And very softly, in his rough-edged, long-unused voice, he began to hum a tune. Jamie recognized it with a shiver. It was Josef's carol.

The deep, rough voice gathered strength and found the shape of the words, and then Josef was singing as well, his clear alto blending perfectly with the old man's bass. Without conscious intention, Jamie found that he himself had joined in, leaning against the doorway with closed eyes and smelling the ancient, damp reek of stone and fern and peaty earth. The voices soared and he no longer noticed the scream of the wind outside. In the privacy of his own darkness, the building was truly a cathedral, and a great chorus took up the theme in a rich body of sound and carried it, amid a blaze of candlelight and the smoke of incense, up into the dark roof and beyond it to the everlasting sky.

When it ended, Jamie gave a shuddering sigh. He opened his eyes and saw that the old man was standing at the far end of the building with his arms outstretched as if he stood in reverence before an altar. Slowly he turned and smiled at Jamie. 'Now,' he said. 'We must go.'

The crashing of trees seemed to break upon them like a gathering peal of thunder. Instinctively Jamie flung up his arms to protect his head. He was flung backwards by a violence which hurled him out of the doorway and left him sprawled in the wet grass.

Half-stunned, he lay there for a few moments until the cold rain in his face made him realize that this was not a nightmare. Something terrible really had happened. He scrambled up and rubbed his eyes on his anorak sleeve.

Then he saw it.

The building had been axed across by the fallen walnut tree which, in its turn, had been crushed by the collapsing weight of two or three others which had stood above it, up the hill. They had come crashing down like huge, toppling dominoes, each felling the next. The massive trunk of the walnut tree had plunged into the disintegrating roof, dislodging the upper stones of the wall to cut deeply into the cathedral's interior.

Jamie fought his way over the mass of branches, back into the shattered building. The old man lay pinned below a heavy limb of the tree, but his eyes were open, looking at Jamie. 'It's all right,' he said. And the voice with which he spoke was easy and light. It was Josef's voice.

Desperately, Jamie pushed at the crushing weight of the tree. It was useless. He felt as insignificant as an insect.

The old man smiled, but his eyes did not seem to be looking at Jamie any more. His lips moved, and Jamie bent close to hear the last, light whisper of Josef's voice. 'It really is all right. I told you.'

And then Jamie knew he was alone. A great sob welled up in his chest. He got to his feet and looked down through his tears at the outflung arm and the white hair of the man who lay at his feet, and whose face was so empty. He was not a person any more. He had gone, and Josef had gone with him.

Jamie turned and ran. Slipping and sliding, he crashed through the

bushes and across the burn. Once out on the hill, he ran full tilt through the bracken and heather in the pouring rain. Blinded by his tears, he fell heavily as he caught his foot in a thick loop of bramble, but he picked himself up and ran on. From the house below him, he could hear his mother calling his name. And the visiting woman was calling, too. 'Joe!' she cried, and her voice was snatched away by the wind which tore the clouds to rags in the darkening sky. 'Joe! Where are you? Josef!'

Jamie made no further protest about the sale of the house. Mrs Pringle's interest in it was demolished by the accident, but it was sold the following spring to a couple returning to Scotland after some years spent in New Zealand, and Jamie's parents bought the house they had coveted, conveniently close to the High School.

They were not entirely sure that the move was a success. Since the accident, Jamie had been silent and reserved. They were relieved to see that he had given up talking to his invisible companion, but it worried them that the boy hardly spoke at all unless prompted very insistently. He never left the house except to go obediently to school, where Miss Mayhew reported that he sat with his hands in his lap and did nothing more than obey any instruction he was explicitly given.

Jamie gazed his way indifferently through a summer holiday in Malta and then began at the High School, where his total apathy and silence caused him to be classified as educationally subnormal.

One day in late November, almost exactly a year after the accident, Jamie followed the rest of his class into Mr McKenzie's music room. The master watched them with tolerant exasperation as the small group of children muddled its way into sitting in a semi-circle of chairs as instructed. It was no use expecting much of this lot, he told himself. Poor wee souls. One had to be patient.

Jamie sat down with his hands in his lap and gazed at the pattern of things which his eyes half-saw. There were the shapes of people moving about, and a larger one standing up. Light came in through the big windows. He quite liked the light. There was nothing else to like, now Josef had gone. A part of Jamie had gone with him, into candlelight and incense and a ragged sky, living on in the time when he had not been alone.

Mr McKenzie sat down at the piano and struck a chord. 'Now,' he said when the children were quieter, 'all the first-years are going to learn a new carol for Christmas. New to us, that is. It's a very old carol, really—a traditional one from Russia. Listen while I play it through.'

He glanced at the group of children as he played, and was startled to see Jamie White leaning forward with lips parted in an eager smile. He looked transfigured. 'Sing it, Jamie, if you know it,' Mr McKenzie suggested. He had no real expectation that the boy would attempt to sing, but, to his astonishment, Jamie's voice rose easily in the carol, the pattern of words unrolling from his memory, oblivious of his classmates' giggles.

'Good gracious me,' said Mr McKenzie as he brought the music to its close. 'That was great, Jamie. And you know the Russian words, too. Where did you learn those?'

Jamie's eagerness was fading. He cradled his hands in his lap and looked away out of the window. 'It's Josef's carol,' he said unwillingly. It was the first time the teacher had heard him speak.

'Josef.' Mr McKenzie tried to make sense of this. 'Joseph and Mary, do you mean?'

The boy did not even shake his head. His blue-eyed gaze took in Mr McKenzie's presence, but, as usual, without any recognition, as if the man was a part of the chair on which he sat. Mr McKenzie gave up. 'Right,' he said to the class in general, 'now listen to the first three notes and sing them after me.'

The carol came strangely to Jamie's ears, broken and disjointed. He shook his head irritably, wanting the music to flow on, wanting to be transported back to the lovely wholeness of Josef's voice drifting up to the dark roof and beyond it to the sky. He blinked and frowned as the children stumbled again through the first phrase of the song. What had Josef said about the feeling which music brought? 'It is part of the everlasting light.'

The class sang another line of the carol, inaccurately. Jamie scowled. The sound they made was intensely irritating, and it broke through into the silence which Josef had left. He could not shut it out. He fidgeted crossly. Why couldn't they get it right?

Outside, a faint November sun sparkled across the pale sea. Jamie craned his neck to look at it, noticing how the flecks of light were in constant movement. The bare trees in the school garden were motionless, their branches making an intricate tracery across the white sky. Everything out there was full of light. It was something to do with what Josef had meant. Jamie stood up as the class sang another ragged phrase.

'Sit down, Jamie,' said Mr McKenzie.

The boy's eyes met his in a perfectly rational communication. 'If you wouldn't mind,' he said politely, 'I'd like to go outside. I'll come back.'

The class snorted with amusement and Mr McKenzie looked startled. He hesitated. 'You promise?' he asked.

'Of course,' said Jamie with dignity.

There was a longer pause, then Mr McKenzie made up his mind. 'All right,' he said. 'But don't be long.'

Jamie left the room.

Almost unwillingly, he felt a new awareness of what his surroundings were like. As he walked down the corridor, he stared at the wavy pattern of the vinyl floor and heard the distant ranting of a teacher scolding her class for some misdemeanour. He read the words of the posters about Youth Training Schemes and remembered that other time of acute awareness when he had leaned, panting and hot, against the doorway of the cathedral, and heard Josef singing.

He went through the double doors into the foyer and looked intently at the brickwork of the modern hexagonal pillars, and at the sliding glass window of the secretary's office. There was a crumpled crisp bag beside the leg of a blue-upholstered chair. He pushed open the glass door and went out.

A flock of gulls flew up from the sea and wheeled away across the pale sky, and Jamie smiled. Faintly, the untidy voices of the class brought fragments of the carol to his ears. Like painful little pins, they connected this reality to the existence of Josef. 'You're everywhere,' Jamie said to the sky. He was acutely aware of the cold air which went in and out of his lungs, and of the screaming gulls, of the faint, salty reek of the sea and of the way the sky was cut into multi-shaped segments by the black branches of the trees. Josef was in all of them. He knew now what his friend had meant. It was all right.

Jamie turned to go back to the music room. Perhaps he'd better help them get the carol right, he thought. And he'd have to learn the English words. Josef wouldn't mind.

Mary's Story
Margrit Cruickshank

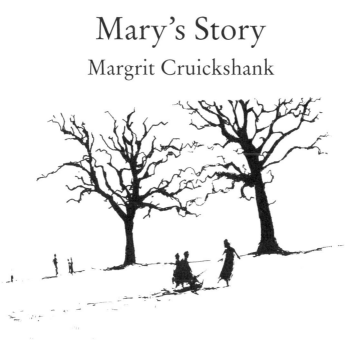

THE only ghost story I know is a real one. It happened to a friend of mine a long time ago.

Mary and I grew up in a remote village. Her father was the village schoolmaster and their house, along with the local doctor's and the manse, was one of the biggest in the village: an old granite house (the date 1711 was carved on a worn stone plaque above the front door), whose passageways, stairs, and corners were ideal for games of hide-and-seek, and whose walls were so thick that you could curl up in the seats in the window ledges and read or daydream to your heart's content. It was full of old furniture and dark pictures in heavy gilded frames, some of which had belonged to Mary's family for hundreds of years. Our family was just a blow-in by comparison.

A rowan tree grew outside Mary's window, planted a great many years ago—as had been the custom then—to keep witches at bay. In windy weather it would knock at her window-pane with scratchy fingertips, scaring me half to death if I was staying overnight. Mary didn't mind it: to her the tree's sighing and whispering was that of an old familiar friend.

In summer, the village and its surrounding countryside was an inviting playground of gardens, fields, moor, and river. But in winter the same countryside was under a magic spell. The sharp edges of walls and bushes were softened by a smooth blanket of snow, the rushing brown river, in whose shallows Mary and I had, just a few months earlier, paddled and caught minnows in jamjars, was tamed by a thick uneven layer of ice; icicles hung from wizened bracken fronds and glinted like crystal pendants in the cold sunlight; skeletal trees were rimed with white frost; the firs and pines bore deep cushions of snow on their branches; and the air was so sharp and clear that the voices of us children, sledging on the hill, carried for miles.

Winters in that part of the world were fierce. The snow started in November and lasted till March. But people were used to it. They cleared their paths, kept their fires blazing and visited the old and infirm to see that they lacked for nothing.

It was in winter that the events in this story took place.

The previous autumn, Mary's mother had been expecting a new baby. One day Mary was sent round to our house with permission to stay the night. It was one of those marvellous sunny days you sometimes get in late autumn and we spent the afternoon picking blackberries, elderberries, and rosehips and then helping my mother to boil the fruit in our huge aluminium jam pan, pour it through the jelly bag and finally fill jar after jar with translucent, purple-black hedgerow jelly.

In the morning, Mary had a new sister: Elizabeth.

Elizabeth was a sickly child. She caught every cold that was going. It was pitiful to see her little chest heave as she tried to breathe and hear her shrill insistent crying. Mary's mother was worried—and was short-tempered with Mary and myself. Especially when the weather got colder and the snow came.

In previous years, she had cheerfully helped us to make snowmen and igloos in the schoolhouse garden, or had put on wellington boots and pulled us on the heavy wooden sledge—our feet held up out of the snow and our breath steaming in the cold, sharp air—along the road to the hill behind Black's farm where the best sledging was. Now, she complained when we dragged wet footsteps into the house or left the door open by mistake or gave her yet another pair of mitts soaked by snowball-making to be dried. We took to spending more time at my house instead.

Mind you, Elizabeth wasn't always sick. Sometimes she was well for weeks and sometimes, if the sun was shining and the air so crisp it burned the back of your throat, we were allowed to wrap her up and take her outside. One of us would sit on the sledge, with Elizabeth (smothered in baby blankets like an Eskimo) in her lap, while the other would play the husky dog and pull the sledge around the garden. Elizabeth loved it!

She was beautiful, Elizabeth. She wasn't bald like some babies but had fine black hair, her eyes were blue and her little nose turned up at the end. And, when she wasn't crying, she had this really incredible smile: as if seeing you was the best thing that had ever happened to her. But the most amazing thing about her was her fingers. They were so small and so perfect, with three little joints on each and tiny pearly fingernails. She loved to grab your finger and would hold on much more tightly than you'd ever imagine such a tiny thing would be capable of.

Anyway, it had been snowing as usual through November and December; nothing very special, nothing we couldn't cope with. And then, on Christmas Eve, the blizzard started. It snowed non-stop all day, blinding, driving snow which piled up against walls and bushes and caused drifts which kept us inside from early morning on. By the afternoon the flakes were so thick that they obliterated everything outside the windows in a swirling, dancing curtain of white. The wind, which had been rising all day, now howled around the corners of the house and screamed down the chimney, making the parlour fire choke and cough black smoke into the room.

'If it gets any worse, I doubt if Santa will be able to get out with his reindeer tonight,' my father joked.

Seeing our faces, Mother smiled reassuringly. 'He's got Rudolph,' she told Dad. 'He's always got through until now. I wouldn't worry.'

But it wasn't Rudolph and Santa Claus that they were worrying about at the schoolhouse that night.

Elizabeth had fallen sick again. Dr Frankland had come in the morning and given her some medicine: if she wasn't better in twenty-four hours, he had said, Mary's parents should get back to him, 'Christmas Day or no Christmas Day.'

She didn't get better, she got worse. By evening, Mary's mother decided to call in Dr Frankland again.

She dialled his number, but the phone didn't work. A tree must have blown over in the blizzard and pulled the phone lines down with it.

'I'll go and get Bill,' Mary's father said, referring to Dr Frankland.

Mary's mother pulled back the curtain in her living room and looked out into the night. Snow was still falling, the wind still howling, and the snowflakes in front of the window reflected back the light from the house like a dense, impenetrable wall. 'You can't go out in that,' she said.

'Of course I can.'

Mary's dad took his thick winter coat from the coat rack, settled his tweed cap firmly over his ears, wrapped a muffler around his neck and pulled galoshes over his shoes. He took her grandad's old walking stick from the umbrella stand and opened the front door.

The snow, laying siege to the house like a threatening army, tried to force an entry in a flurry of wet, white flakes. Mary, sheltering behind her mother, looked out: she couldn't even see the bushes at the side of the garden path, let alone the gate into the village street. The drift up against the door had completely covered all the front steps and was forming a ledge, already six inches high, across the doorway.

Mary's mother put out a hand to hold him back, but it was too late: he pushed his way out into the whiteness and shut the door firmly behind him.

'Pray God he'll be all right,' Mary's mother said. And then Elizabeth cried again from the nursery upstairs and she ran to comfort her.

The evening wore on. It was long past Mary's bedtime, but neither of them thought of it. And neither of them thought of Santa Claus either, despite the stockings hung up from the drawing-room mantelpiece and the tree covered in tinsel and glass baubles.

Finally, Elizabeth's cries eased off and Mary's mother came downstairs. 'She's sleeping now, thank goodness. Let's hope the crisis is over.'

Mary went into the kitchen and made tea from the kettle simmering on the big Aga stove. They sat side by side in front of the drawing-room fire, thinking of Mary's father, out there in the blizzard, trying to plough his way through snowdrifts to the doctor's house. In both their minds was the fear that he might lose his sense of direction in the white-out, might even now be lying in the ditch, giving up the fight against the cold, drifting into sleep. (In that part of the world, everybody knows how dangerous this is and how, so easily, you can give in to death.)

They sipped their tea and thought of this, but neither of them spoke.

Eventually Mary's mother looked up. 'You'd better go up to bed, love.' She tried to smile. 'It's Christmas Day tomorrow.'

Mary snuggled up closer to her mother on the sofa. 'Can't I stay up for a little while longer?'

Until Dad comes home, she meant.

'No, love. Up you go.'

Unwillingly, Mary climbed upstairs to her bedroom. The baby's nursery was at the top of the stairs. It had once been Mary's grandmother's room: the old double bed had been pushed to one side and was piled with towels, nappies, tiny baby clothes, and all the other paraphernalia a baby needs. Although a bright twirling mobile of multi-coloured fish hung above Elizabeth's cot, the room was dominated by an old family portrait on the wall beside the window. From it, a youngish woman in old-fashioned clothes looked down at Elizabeth's cot. She was very pretty, the lady in the picture, and had a kind smile on her face. Mary claimed that she was her great-great-great-grandmother and that everybody said that she, Mary, took after her. I couldn't see it myself though.

Sometimes, when we were in the nursery changing Elizabeth or putting her down to sleep, we would look at the portrait and play a game, thinking of more and more reasons why the lady should be smiling. Was she in love with an artist who had painted her picture? we wondered. Maybe they were star-crossed lovers and she had run away with him one dark and moonless night?

'She can't have done,' Mary objected. 'She wouldn't be my great-great-great-granny if she'd run off with somebody else.'

'The artist could be your great-great-great-grandad?' I suggested. 'It's a shame you didn't inherit any of his talent!'

Anyhow, Mary told me later, she decided to look in on Elizabeth before she went to bed. Very quietly, so as not to wake the baby again, she eased open the door. The room was lit by an eerie glow from the snow outside. The picture of the lady was in shadow, but the mobile caught the light from the hall and twinkled as it spun in the draught.

There was no movement from the cot: Elizabeth was asleep.

Mary tiptoed across the room and leant over the cradle. Elizabeth was so sweet, so peaceful, sleeping with her tiny fingers curled up under her chin and her black hair falling gently over her little white face. Her tears had dried and she wasn't gasping for breath any more. In fact, she hardly seemed to be breathing at all.

Mary felt a cold hand drive through her chest to clench around her heart. 'Elizabeth!' she whispered urgently. 'Bethie! Wake up!'

The baby didn't move. She lay there, as beautiful and as still as a porcelain doll.

'Mummy!' Mary tried to scream but no words came out of her mouth. It was as if she'd been turned into a statue of ice, she said, as if the snow witch in a fairy tale had cast a spell on her. Finally she managed to break free and rush to the door. 'Mummy!' she tried to call again.

And then something made her turn round. She didn't know what. 'It was weird,' she told me afterwards. 'Like a great power of peace in the room behind me. I mean, outside, the wind was still howling, I could even hear the rowan tree banging at the window in my room across the landing, as if it was trying to knock down the house; but behind me, in Elizabeth's room there was a calmness like . . . I don't know, like as if the world had stopped and was just waiting for something to happen.'

'Weren't you terrified?' I asked.

But she hadn't been. That was the amazing thing. She hadn't been scared at all. She had turned and looked back into the room.

What happened next I find very difficult to believe. But Mary told it to me, just as I'm going to tell you. And Mary wasn't the sort of girl to make up stories. Or rather, she would make up stories all right, but she never pretended her made-up stories were real. And this was real, she said, 'As real as I'm standing here now.'

When she looked back into the room, a lady was bending over Elizabeth's cot, just as Mary herself had bent over it moments before. The lady didn't seem to be aware that Mary was there.

She picked Elizabeth up out of the cot and cradled her in her arms, looking down at her with a gentle, sad smile.

Mary watched, unable to do or say anything. 'It wasn't as if I even thought whether the woman was going to hurt Elizabeth or not. I mean, it was just so obvious to me that she wasn't. I didn't even wonder any more whether Elizabeth was alive or dead: I just knew, somehow, that she was all right. Even if she was dead, everything was all right.'

The woman held Elizabeth for a few seconds (a few minutes? Mary had no idea) and then laid her gently back down into the cot.

'She seemed to fade, then,' Mary said. 'I hadn't thought of looking at the picture before. When I did, it was just like it ought to be, with the woman, great-great-great granny, in it. Looking as if she'd never left it.'

('And it *was* your great-great-great grandmother at the cot?' I asked every time.

'Yes.'

'How can you be so sure? You've said yourself you didn't put on the light. It must have been nearly dark.'

'It was her. Anyway, who else could it have been?')

Mary didn't know how long she stood there. She became aware of someone pounding at the front door. She jumped at the noise, she says, and then ran over to Elizabeth's cot. Elizabeth was breathing! Breathing raggedly, but definitely breathing!

As Mary raced downstairs, the hall door opened and her father and Dr Frankland staggered in, brushing drifts of snow from their coats, shaking snow off their caps, banging their hands together to get warm.

'I'll go straight upstairs,' Dr Frankland said as soon as he'd got off his coat and his galoshes.

Mary stood aside on the stairs to let him past.

'And that's the end of the story,' she told me. 'Elizabeth was sick all over Christmas but she survived, and she's never been really ill since. And Santa came after all, despite the blizzard. That was the year I got my first ice skates, remember?'

'What about your great-whatever grandmother in the painting?' I asked. 'Did she ever walk again?'

'No,' Mary said. 'Why would she?'

It's a funny thing: I believed Mary, but I can't believe in ghosts. Not even after that. But maybe there are more things in heaven and earth, as Hamlet said, than are dreamt of in my philosophy.

Who knows? I certainly don't.

The Adventuress

Frank O'Connor

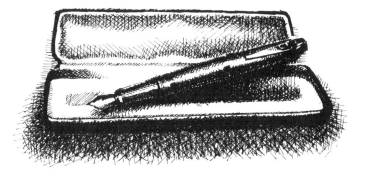

MY brother and sisters didn't really like Brenda at all but I did. She was a couple of years older than I was and I was devoted to her. She had a long, grave, bony face and a power of concealing her real feelings about everything, even about me. I knew she liked me but she wasn't exactly what you'd call demonstrative about it. In fact there were times you might even say she was vindictive.

That was part of her toughness. She was tough to the point of foolhardiness. She would do anything a boy would do and a lot of things that few boys would do. It was never safe to dare her to anything. Someone had only to say 'Brenda, you wouldn't go up and knock at that door' and if the fancy took her Brenda would do it and when the door was opened concoct some preposterous yarn about being up from the country for the day and having lost her way which sometimes even took in the people she called on. When someone once asked if she could ride a bicycle she replied that she could and almost proved her case by falling under a milk-van. She did the same thing with horses and when at last she managed to break her collar-bone she took it with the stoicism of a Red Indian. She would chance her arm at anything and as a result she became not only daring but skilful. She developed into a really stylish horsewoman.

Of course to the others she was just a liar, a chancer, and a notice-box and in return she proved a devil to them. But to me who was always prepared to concede how wonderful she was, she was the soul of generosity.

'Go on,' she would say sharply, handing me a bag of sweets or a fistful of coppers. 'Take the blooming lot. I don't want them.' I suspect now that all she really wanted was admiration, for she would give the shift off her back to anyone she liked. Like all natural aristocrats she found the rest of the world so far beneath her own standards that all were equal in her eyes and she associated with the most horrid children whose allegiance she bought with sweets or cigarettes—pinched off my brother Colum most of the time.

She got away with a lot because she was my father's favourite and knew it. The old man was tall, gaunt, and temperamental. He might pass you for weeks without noticing your existence except when you happened to be doing something wrong. We were all in a conspiracy against him—even Mother, who rationalized it on the plea that we mustn't worry poor Dad. When eventually there were things to worry about (like Colum taking to the bottle or Brenda heaving herself at the commercial traveller's head) the suspicion of all the things we were concealing from him in order not to worry him, finally nearly drove the old man to an early grave.

The rest of us went in fear and trembling of him, but Brenda could cheek him to his face and get away with it and to give her her due she never allowed any of us to criticize him in front of her. Oedipus complex or something I suppose that was.

One year she took it into her head that we should give him a Christmas box as we gave Mother one.

'Why would we give him a Christmas box?' asked Colum suspiciously. 'He never does anything for us.'

'Well,' said Brenda, 'how can we expect him to be any different when we make distinctions between Mother and him? Anyway, only for him we wouldn't be here at all.'

'I don't see that that's any good reason for giving him a Christmas box,' said Colum who was at the age when he was rather inclined to look on it as a grievance. 'What would you give him?'

'We could give him a fountain pen,' said Brenda who had it all pat. 'The one he had he lost three years ago.'

'We could,' said Colum ironically. 'Or a new car.'

'You needn't be so blooming mean,' snapped Brenda. 'Rooney's have grand pens for ten and a tanner. What is it, only two bob a man?'

There was some friction between Brenda and Maeve as to which of them should be Treasurer and Colum supported Maeve only because he knew she was a fanciful sort of girl who would get out of a Grand National Appeal in imitation print and then bother her head no further about it; but Brenda realized that this was sabotage and made short work of it. The idea was hers and she was going to be President, Treasurer, and Secretary—and God help anyone that got in the way.

Two bob a man was reasonable enough, even allowing for another present for Mother. Coming on to Christmas we all got anything up to ten bob a man from relatives up from the country for the Christmas shopping and Brenda watched us with an eye like a hawk so that before Christmas Eve came at all she had collected the subscriptions. I was allowed to go into town with her to make the purchase and seeing that I was her faithful vassal she blew three and six of her own money on an air-gun for me. That was the sort Brenda was.

We went into Rooney's which was a combined book and stationery shop and I was amazed at her self-possession.

'I want to have a look at a few fountain pens,' she said to a gawky-looking assistant called Coakley who lived up our road. He gaped at us across the counter. I could see he liked Brenda.

'Certainly, miss,' he said and I nearly burst with reflected glory to hear her called 'miss'. She took it calmly enough as though she had never been called anything else. 'What sort of pen would you like?'

'Show us a few,' she said with a queenly toss of the head.

'If you want something really first-class,' said Coakley, producing a couple of trays of pens from the glass-case, 'there's the best on the market. Of course, we have the cheaper ones as well but they're not the same at all.'

'How much is this one?' asked Brenda, looking at the one he had pointed out to us.

'Thirty bob,' said Coakley. 'That's a Walker. 'Tis a lot of money of course but 'tis worth it.'

'They all look much alike to me,' said Brenda, taking up one of the cheaper ones.

'Aha!' said Coakley with a guffaw. 'They're only got up like that to take in the mugs.'

Then he threw himself across the counter, took a fountain pen from his own breast pocket and removed the cap. 'See that pen?' he said. 'Guess how long I have that!'

'I couldn't,' said Brenda.

'Fifteen years!' said Coakley. 'Fifteen blooming years. I had it through the war, in jail and everything. I did every blessed thing to that pen only stop a bullet with it. That's a Walker for you! There isn't another pen in the market you could say the same about.' He looked at it fondly, screwed back the cap and returned it to his pocket. You could see he was very fond of that pen.

'Give it to us for a quid!' said Brenda.

'A quid?' he exclaimed, taken aback by her coolness. 'You might as well ask me to give it to you for a present.'

'Don't be so blooming mean,' said Brenda sharply. 'What's ten bob one way or another to ye?'

'Tell me,' said Coakley, raising his hand to his mouth and speaking in a husky whisper. 'Do you know Mr Rooney?'

'No,' said Brenda. 'Why?'

'You ought to go and ask him that,' guffawed Coakley behind his hand. 'Cripes!' he exploded. 'I'd love to see his face.'

'Anyway,' said Brenda, seeing that this line was a complete washout, 'you can split the difference. I'd give you thirty bob but I'm after blowing three and six on an air-gun for the kid. I'll give you twenty-five bob.'

'And will you give me two pound ten a week after I'm sacked?' asked Coakley indignantly.

Even then I thought Brenda would take the dearer pen even if it meant throwing in my air-gun to make up the price. I could see how it hurt her pride to offer my father anything that wasn't of the very best.

'All right so,' she said, seeing no other way out. 'I'll take the one for ten and a tanner. It looks good enough anyway.'

'Ah, 'tis all right,' said Coakley, relenting and trying to put things in the best light. 'As a matter of fact, 'tis quite a decent little pen at the price. We're selling dozens of them.'

But Brenda wasn't consoled at all. The very way he said 'a decent little pen' in that patronizing tone reduced it to mediocrity and pettiness in her eyes while the fact that others beside herself were buying it put the finishing touch to it. She stood on the wet pavement when we emerged with a brooding look in her eyes.

'I was a fool to go near Coakley,' she said at last.

'Why, Brenda?' I asked.

'He never took his eyes off us the whole time. Only for that I'd have fecked one of the decent pens.'

'But you wouldn't do that, Brenda?' I said aghast.

'Why wouldn't I?' she retorted roughly. 'Haven't they plenty of them? If I had the thirty bob I'd have bought it,' she added. 'But that gang is so mean they wouldn't even thank me for it. They think I'm going to offer Daddy a cheap old pen as if that was all we thought of him.'

'What are you going to do?' I asked.

'I'll do something,' she replied darkly.

That was one of the joys of being with Brenda. When I came to an obstacle I howled till someone showed me how to get round it, but Brenda saw three separate ways round it before she came to it at all. Coakley had given us a nice box for the pen. The price was pencilled on the box and when we got home Brenda rubbed it out and replaced it with a neat '30s'. She smiled at my look of awe.

'But won't he know, Brenda?' I asked.

'How would he know?' replied Brenda with a shrug. 'They all look exactly alike.'

That was the sort of thing which made life with her a continuous excitement. She didn't give the matter another thought, but I kept looking forward to Christmas morning, half in dread my father would find her out, half in expectation that Brenda would get away with it again.

In our house we didn't go in much for Christmas trees. At breakfast on Christmas morning Maeve gave Mother a brooch and Brenda gave Daddy the little box containing the pen.

'Hallo!' he said in surprise. 'What's this?' Then he opened it and saw.

'Oh, that's very nice,' he said with real enthusiasm. 'That's the very thing I was wanting this long time. Which of ye thought of that?'

'Brenda did,' I said promptly, seeing that the others would be cut in pieces before they gave her the credit.

'That was very nice and thoughtful of you, Brenda,' said my father, making, for him, a remarkably gracious speech. 'Very nice and thoughtful and I'm sure I'm grateful to ye all. How much did you pay for it?'

(That was more like Daddy!)

'I think the price is on the box,' said Brenda nonchalantly.

'Thirty bob!' said my father, impressed in spite of himself and I looked at the faces of Colum, Maeve, and Brigid and saw that they were impressed too, in a different way. They were wondering what tricks Brenda was up to now. 'Where did you get it?' he went on.

'Rooney's,' replied Brenda.

'Rooney's?' repeated my father suspiciously as he unscrewed the cap and examined the nib. 'Ah, they saw you coming! Sure, Rooney's have Walker pens for thirty bob!'

'I know,' said Brenda hastily. 'We looked at them too but we didn't think much of them. The assistant didn't think much of them either. Isn't that right, Michael?'

'That's right,' I said loyally. 'Them were the best.'

'*They* were the best, dear,' said Mother.

'Ah,' said my father, growing more suspicious than ever. 'That assistant was only taking you out for a walk. Which of them was it? Coakley?'

'No,' said Brenda quickly before I could reply. 'A fellow I never saw there before.'

'Hah!' said my father darkly. 'I'd be surprised if Coakley did a thing like that. That's terrible blackguarding,' he added hotly to Mother. 'Willie Rooney trying to get rid of his trash on people that don't know better. I have a good mind to go in and tell him so. Jerry Taylor in the yard has a Walker pen that he bought ages ago and 'tis still good for a lifetime.'

'Ah, why would you worry yourself about it?' said Mother comfortably. She probably suspected that there was mischief behind, and in her usual way wanted to keep it from Father.

'Oh,' said my father querulously, 'I'd like to show Willie Rooney he can't treat me like that. I'll tell you what you'll do, Brenda,' he said, putting the pen back in the box and returning it to her. 'Put that away carefully till Thursday and then take it back to Rooney's. Have nothing to say to any of the other assistants but go straight to Coakley and tell him I sent you. Say you want a Walker in exchange for that and no palaver about it. He'll see you're not codded again.'

I will say for Brenda that her face never changed. She had a wonderful way of concealing her emotions. But the fury among the family afterwards was something terrible.

'Ah,' said Maeve indignantly, 'you're always the same, out for nothing only swank and grandeur.'

'I wouldn't mind the swank and grandeur only for the lies,' said Colum. 'One of these days you'll be getting yourself into serious trouble. I suppose you didn't know you could be had up for that. Changing the prices on boxes is the same thing as forgery. You could get the jail for that.'

'All right,' said Brenda contemptuously. 'Let them give me the jail. Now, I want to know what I'm to do to make up the extra quid.'

'Make it up yourself,' snapped Maeve. ''Twas your notion and you can pay for it.'

'I can't,' said Brenda with a shrug. 'I haven't it.'

'Then you can go and find it,' said Colum.

'I'll find it all right,' said Brenda, her eyes beginning to flash. 'Either ye give me the extra four bob a man or I'll go in and tell my old fellow that 'twas ye persuaded me to change the price.'

'Go on, you dirty cheat!' said Maeve.

'Oh, leave her do it,' said Colum. 'Leave her do it and see will he believe her.'

'Maybe you think I wouldn't?' asked Brenda with cold ferocity.

Colum had gone too far and he knew it. It was always in the highest degree unsafe to challenge Brenda to do anything, because there was nothing you could positively say Brenda would not do if the fancy took her, and if the fancy did take her there was nothing you could positively say my father wouldn't be prepared to believe. I knew she was doing wrong but still I couldn't help admiring her. She looked grand standing there with the light of battle in her eyes.

'Come on!' she snapped. 'Four bob I want and I'm jolly well going to get it. It's no use pretending ye haven't got it because I know ye have.'

There was a moment's pause. I could see they were afraid.

'Give it to her,' said Colum contemptuously. 'And don't talk to her again, any of ye. She's beneath ye.'

He took out some money, threw two two-shilling pieces on the table and walked out. After a moment Maeve and Bridget did the same in silence. Then I put my hand in my pocket and took out what money I had. It wasn't much.

'Are you going to walk out on me too?' Brenda asked with a mocking smile.

'You know I wouldn't do that,' I said in confusion.

'That's all right so,' she said with a shrug. 'Keep your old money. I had it all the time and I'd have paid it too if only that gang had the decency to stick by me when I was caught.' Her smile grew bitterer and for a second or two I thought she might cry. I had never seen her cry. 'The trouble about our family, Michael,' she went on, 'is that they all have small minds. You're the only one that hasn't. But you're only a baby, and I suppose you'll grow up just like the rest.'

I thought it was very cruel of her to say that and I after standing up for her and all. But Brenda was like that.

The Kissing Gate
John Gordon

THEY wanted him downstairs. They always did. Two days to Christmas, and there was no need to get up this early but his two younger brothers were shaking his shoulder and crying, 'Wake up, Will! Wake up—we want to go down to the stream!'

Mistletoe. That's what they were after. At the spot where they built dams in summer an old apple tree leant over the stream and it was heavy with mistletoe. Every year they collected it and their father took the mistletoe harvest to market for them.

But Will was tired and the thought of getting dressed, trudging through the frosty village to the meadow beyond the bridge and then getting his feet wet in the bend of the stream where the tree was hidden made him hunch his shoulders and press his face into the warm pillow. But the pillow surprised him. It was ridged and hard and prickled his skin as if all the feathers were pushing their quills into his face. He snorted and pawed his muzzle like a fox or a cat and opened his eyes.

It was then that he saw the girl. Or rather, her feet, and then the hem of her long dress, and then slowly upwards until he saw her face, but quite dimly, partly because the light had faded but also because his vision was obscured by some sort of mesh in front of his eyes. He sat up suddenly, and the mesh turned out to be a web of straw stems that had been pricking his skin, and he shivered.

'I should think so, too,' she said. 'If I hadn't found you here you'd have frozen to death.'

He stood up. He was not in bed. He was nowhere near his bed. He ignored the girl and looked around. He was at the foot of a stack of straw bales at the edge of a field that sloped away to the village below. He and the girl were near the lonely church at the top of the hill. And it was not morning. It was a winter twilight.

He knew where he was but he was struggling to discover how he had got there. 'I must have fallen asleep,' he said.

'That's obvious. You were curled up in a ball like little Boy Blue asleep in the meadow.'

'He wasn't in the meadow.' At least by contradicting her he was fighting the confusion that surrounded him. 'It was the sheep who were in meadow.'

She mocked him, bleating like a sheep, except that her girl's voice made it sound more like a lamb.

'Little Bo-peep,' he said.

'Little Boy Blue,' she retorted.

And they both laughed. Her dark hair was made darker by the dusk and her face was a secret, but her voice had a faint catch in it that would have lured any boy he knew. His brothers, for instance. 'I was dreaming,' he said.

'I suppose you live down there.' She pointed down the swell of the hill to where a few pinpricks of light showed where the houses had been swallowed by the darkness. 'You're a village boy.'

He dipped his head. Was he supposed to be ashamed of living in a cottage? He drew in his breath to speak but sleep still clung to him and quite suddenly he did not have the energy to argue. And she was too beautiful to contradict. Just the pale shape of her face told him that. And that strange, lovely voice.

'Where do you come from?' he asked.

She turned away and for a moment he utterly lost sight of her as her dark clothes blended with the shadows. 'Over there,' she said, and now he was able to make out her shape once more and her pale hand pointing towards the black hedge of the churchyard.

He said nothing. Between seeming to wake up in bed and then waking again in the strawstack the whole day had gone. Now it was a cold night, and close to Christmas, but his mind spun into a panic as he suddenly realized he was not sure even of that. And now, when the girl turned towards him, he could barely see her.

'I come from over there,' she repeated, raising her arm to point again. 'Don't you believe me?'

He was slow to answer. 'I've never seen you before.'

'I know that.' Her voice was so low it could have been a breeze whispering through the black hedge, except that the winter air was utterly still. 'And I woke you up and confused you. Poor old you, I gave you a fright.'

Poor old you. He had begun to doubt what he was seeing, but these were hardly the words of a ghost. 'You don't frighten me,' he said, and she laughed.

'I should think not!' She put out a hand. 'Come with me. I'll show you where I belong.' He reached to take her hand, but in the darkness their fingers failed to meet and he felt no more than the cold air as she turned and he followed her to where the hedge arched into the short tunnel that led into the churchyard. He lost sight of her in the blackness and must have blundered past her for when he emerged into the churchyard she was not there.

He stood among the gravestones and looked around, and it was then that old, familiar things began to look real again. The church on the hill was so little used that parts of it were in danger of crumbling. He remembered that, of course he did, but he had not seen the posts and rope that now prevented anyone getting too close to the tower. Then he saw that the posts were new, and it was true it was some time since he had been anywhere near the church. And his memory was not really so bad because he clearly remembered his mother chasing them all out of the house to stop them 'getting under her feet' while she was so busy with the preparations for Christmas. He had helped cut down the mistletoe before he wandered away to escape the clamour of his young brothers.

It had not been very clever of him to fall asleep, but now that he remembered doing it all was well. He took a deep breath and said aloud, 'Are you there? I can't see you.'

'Over here.'

He was slightly startled and had to turn around before he saw that one of the dim shapes among the gravestones was the girl. 'I thought you were a ghost,' he said. Darkness made him bold. 'And even if you are I'm still glad I met you.'

'Why?' And when he did not answer she repeated, 'Tell me why you are glad.'

He hesitated and then risked it. 'Because if you are a ghost you're a very pretty one.' She was silent. He had gone too far and she was offended. 'I'm sorry . . .' he realized he did not know her name '. . . whoever you are.'

She came towards him, moving silently between the headstones. 'This is a sad place.' The catch in her voice was close to tears. 'I read some of the gravestones today. Some of the people were very young, and they are here now, in the cold and the dark, and always will be.'

'But you aren't one of them.'

'No,' she said.

'I'm glad.' He was close enough to see her smile. 'But I still don't know where you come from.'

'If you come to the kissing gate I'll show you.' Her sadness had gone and she turned in a flurry of skirts, expecting him to follow.

'Kissing gate? There ain't no kissing gate up here.'

'There ain't?' Once again she was mimicking him. 'Well that's what I call it, anyway. Over there, in the corner.'

He could just make out the fence against the sheep meadow beyond. 'That's not a kissing gate!' Already he knew her well enough to let laughter show in his voice. She wouldn't mind. 'That's a stile, that's what that is.'

'It may be a stile to you, but in my opinion it works even better as a kissing gate.'

'How come?'

She came a step closer and now, for the first time, he saw her clearly. She was even more darkly pretty than he had believed. 'If you really want to know why it's a kissing gate,' she said, and the catch in her voice was enticing, 'I can show you.'

He followed her through the ancient, leaning headstones to the corner of the churchyard and they stood with the wooden step of the stile between them. 'Now do you see?' she said.

He shook his head.

'That's because you are a boy . . .' she held up a hand to prevent him interrupting '. . . and don't tell me girls can't climb stiles, because they can, but it isn't easy for them if they're wearing long dresses.'

She glanced down at her own dress which almost reached the ground. Old-fashioned, he thought, and then just as quickly changed his mind; girls sometimes did wear long dresses. She raised the hem of her skirt an inch or two and looked up. 'So if the boy is anything like a gentleman he offers her his hand, and then . . .' She broke off as if expecting him to do something, but when he simply stood there she became impatient. 'Well even if he doesn't offer to help her she still has to lean right forward to stop her dress catching on the step and then . . .'

He watched as she began to climb the stile, and as she did so she had to lean towards him. 'And then,' she said, 'their heads are very close together . . . aren't they?'

She was close enough for her perfume to reach him and he knew it was that as much as anything else that had drawn him out of sleep.

'So you see,' she said, 'your stile has become a kissing gate.'

He moved towards her but she drew back quickly. 'I suppose you know the Brandons,' she said, tormenting him.

'Of course I do.' Across the meadow the rooftops of Brandon's Farm were still visible against the sky. He knew the old farmer and his wife.

'We are staying there for Christmas,' she said. 'They are my grandparents.'

'I never knew they had a granddaughter.'

'Well that's me.' Once more she bunched her skirts, and this time he was ready when she leant forward, but somehow only the cold air

touched his face as she slipped past him and stood against the top rail
of the stile.

'Shall I see you again?' he asked.

'Maybe.' She hesitated. 'But it will have to be tomorrow night,
Christmas Eve, and that might make it difficult.'

'I can be here.'

'So how can I refuse?' She stepped down on the other side of the
fence. 'But really I should know your name.'

'I'm Will,' he said. 'Will Judd.'

'Will Judd.' She looked beyond him as if she had heard the name
before and was trying to place him. 'Will Judd,' she repeated, and her
eyes wandered towards the church glooming above them. The dark
shape made her suddenly realize where she was and she shuddered.

'It's cold. I'm freezing.' She glanced at him briefly and turned away. 'I've got to get home.' And she vanished into the night.

He was reluctant to leave the churchyard, and his mind remained anchored there as he wandered away as if his thoughts were stringing out behind him and keeping him in touch with the girl. She was strange, that was certain; no ordinary girl would have turned her back so suddenly after having been so friendly. But everything was strange, the night was strange, and he was part of it and that was the strangest of all because now he had wandered downhill and found himself at home in the lobby at the back of the cottage where the coats were kept and had no memory of how he had got there.

He was in darkness, but along the passageway he saw light under the living room door and he could hear his brothers' voices. They were quarrelling.

The two boys had fallen out over mistletoe. 'I told you we needed to bundle it up different,' said David, the small one. 'But you wouldn't listen, would you!'

'You was giving it away, making such great big bundles. That's why I had to split 'em up.'

'And then Dad had to sell two for the price of one. You are mean, you are! Will wouldn't have made them bunches so stingy.'

'Well, he weren't there, was he? And he ain't here now.' Jack was bullying his small brother, who started to snuffle. 'Cry baby!'

Then their mother's voice. 'Hush up, both of you! What's done is done and there's no going back—not now, not ever.'

It was supper time and they were eating. Will was trying to remember the disagreement over the bundles when he heard David say, 'I think I'll leave something for Will when he gets home.'

'You're being stupid again,' said Jack.

'Well, it's Christmas Eve tomorrow and we do it for Father Christmas.'

'It ain't the same for Will,' Jack's voice was softer, 'and you know it.'

There were no more words, merely the scuffle and clatter of plates being gathered and taken to the kitchen. Supper was over. It was much later than Will had thought, but he had no appetite. He was still standing in the dark when he heard his mother.

'Little David,' she said, 'he breaks your heart with the things he comes out with.'

There was a long silence before his father changed the subject. 'Not much to do in the bottom fields today,' he said, 'so the boss asked me to do a bit of clearing up around Hill Church.'

'He should never have sent you!' His mother was indignant, almost afraid. 'You know it isn't safe near that church—you better than anyone.'

'I know, I know.' His father spoke quietly, calming her. 'But I took care, and there's nothing been done around that church for a year, that I know.'

'Except for one place,' said his mother.

His father grunted, agreeing with her. 'But I wasn't thinking o' that in particular,' he said. 'There's the place where that young girl was buried—the Brandons' girl. It looked to me as if someone had been making a bit of an attempt to look after it.'

His mother sighed. 'Other people have their sorrows, too,' she said. 'But that was years and years ago.'

'Aye, that's true enough.' The chair creaked as his father tilted forward to warm his hands at the fire. 'But it's good that folk remember their own.'

'How can they ever forget!' His mother's cry silenced them both.

Will remained where he was. So now he knew. His first thoughts had been true. He had met a ghost. She was the Brandons' girl, dead long ago. The warmth indoors no longer welcomed him. He belonged outside in the bright, cold night with the ghost of the girl.

Soundlessly he left the house and went up the dark hill to the straw bales where the girl had first seen him. The churchyard was empty so he found the hollow in the straw and curled up within it once more. Perhaps she would find him again. The straw closed around him and he slid into a deep sleep.

Daylight came but did not wake him, and if anyone searched for him along the valley no sound reached him. Sleep had closed around Will Judd so completely that all day long he lay in the strawstack and it was not until the weak winter sun slid out of the sky that he stirred.

The torpor that had held him during daylight eased and he came out from the shelter of the stack to look down the slope. The frost lay white along the furrows of the ploughed land, and far below there were a few glimpses of yellow light in the village which gave a hint of the warmth withindoors and the excitements of Christmas Eve. But he thought only of the lonely ghost and turned his back on the village to make his way in the starlight to Anne Brandon's gravestone. Someone had cleared the ivy from its face, just as his father had said, and it must have been that which had disturbed her long sleep.

He stood without moving among the silent congregation of headstones. They were ancient and tired. Some were leaning, tilting their heads together, and many lay asleep, clustered under the dark walls of the church. It was a clear night and his mind was moving among the bright drifts of stars overhead when he heard his name.

'Will Judd!'

It was not spoken loudly, but he could not mistake the voice.

'Is that you, Will Judd?'

He had to search the margins of the churchyard before he saw her. She was on the stile, clinging to the top rail, not yet ready to step down among the gravestones. He went towards her through the frozen grass.

'Can you hear me, Will Judd?' There was an added catch to her voice as though she was afraid of being alone in such a place.

'Of course I can hear you.'

'Will Judd.' She had not heard him. 'If you are there can you come forward?'

She was not as bold as the night before, and he advanced cautiously until he stood beneath the stile, her kissing gate, and he remained silent so as not to disturb her. Still she did not seem to see him but spoke out across the graveyard as if she thought he was near the church.

'When I saw you last night, Will Judd, I did not know who you were until you said your name.'

She paused as if she was waiting for a reply but he stood silently, looking up at the poor ghost, and waited.

'I was going to look at Anne Brandon's grave,' she said, still speaking to the shadows. 'She died so long ago I've been pulling ivy from her gravestone, and last night I felt so sorry for her I just could not keep away.'

A ghost did not pull ivy from a gravestone. Yet the girl had done so. The knowledge that she was no ghost filled his mind. Only the dark night had made her seem so. He opened his mouth to speak, but had to listen.

'Anne Brandon,' said the girl, 'she was my great-great-aunt of long ago and died so young. It was when I was pulling the ivy away that I saw the other headstone.'

She was no ghost. His mind clung to that alone, and he hardly heard what she was saying. 'The other headstone,' she said again, and she caught her breath as though something had distracted her. Her voice sank so low it was little more than a whisper, but he listened. 'It was then I saw your name, Will Judd . . . I saw it on the headstone.'

He let her words vanish on the air. To banish them from his mind he took a step nearer the stile, and at last she saw him. He heard her draw in her breath and he could see that she trembled as she clung to the rail.

'Will Judd?' Her voice was very faint, and although he answered she seemed not to hear. 'I'm sorry, Will, but I didn't know about you until they told me. I just thought you were asleep when I saw you in that strawstack, I didn't know you were . . .'

Her voice failed and he watched as she struggled to continue. And now, for the first time, he was cold. His legs were like lead, too heavy to move. He stood near the foot of his own grave and watched without speaking. Slowly she regained her courage and crossed the stile to stand on the step above him before she spoke again. 'I didn't know what had happened to you, Will. I didn't know that was where they found you . . . in the field.'

He felt nothing. Her words held no surprise. Ever since she had wakened him in the field he had drifted through a daze of half remembering. The cottage where he was born had drawn him back, but only to linger in the dark and listen. Little David had wanted to leave food for him, but the others had known this was useless. He would never be coming back. His mind cleared and he saw himself again on the day he stood at the foot of the church tower looking up as part of the parapet broke loose and blotted out the sky as it fell. And then, knowing he was badly hurt but feeling nothing, he had crawled away, out through the tunnel in the hedge to lie in the straw at the edge of the field.

'That's where I saw you,' she said. 'They found you there.'

The place where he had died.

He was gazing up at her when suddenly, fearfully, she jumped from the stile and stood beside him. 'Will Judd,' she said, 'I'm so sorry for you!' and she bent forward as if to kiss his cheek. He did not feel the touch of her lips and, if she herself felt anything, it was no more than the chill of the night air. And then, scrambling and clumsy in her haste to be away, she turned and climbed back over her kissing gate.

She looked back only once. Under the lightless church windows, where the frozen grasses bent over a fallen headstone, a solitary figure sat gazing into the long night. She turned away and fled towards the glow of the farmhouse windows where Christmas was beginning.

The Carol Singer

Chris Naylor

L AST Christmas Eve was cold and foggy—a dank, unpleasant night, not festive in the least.

I was lazing in an armchair in front of the fire, reading, with a glass of mulled wine at my elbow. I'd eaten the last of the rich Christmas cake I'd been keeping in the larder. I don't stint myself at Christmas, it's a time for warmth and good living.

A shuffling step approached the porch. A solitary male voice, thin and hoarse, began to sing.

> '*God rest ye merry, gentlemen,*
> *Let nothing you dismay . . .*'

He sang every verse, which pleased me. Most carol-singers nowadays get stuck after a few lines. I went to the door and opened it.

'Come inside and have a drink.'

He shuffled in, and sat in the other fireside chair. I gave him some mulled wine, which he drank eagerly. He was thin, very pale, perhaps forty but looking older, with the air of an undernourished bank-clerk. His coarse, heavy greatcoat and woollen muffler almost swallowed him up. And he wore a top-hat, which was distinctly unusual.

He coughed, a rasping, unhealthy sound, and glanced at me

apologetically. 'My lungs; I suffer from bronchitis. I shouldn't really be out on a night like this.'

'So why are you?'

He smiled. 'I like to go carol-singing on Christmas Eve. People are very kind. They often invite me in, give me something warming to drink.' He sipped the mulled wine gratefully, yet it didn't seem to be taking the pallor out of his cheeks. The blazing fire seemed not to warm him, either; he was still hunched in his thick coat as if frozen to the marrow.

We chatted inconsequentially for a while. Eventually he stood up reluctantly.

'I'd better go. I promised myself I'd sing "God rest ye merry" at every house in the street before midnight.' He picked up the top-hat from the table.

'Your clothes,' I observed. 'They're rather old-fashioned, aren't they?'

He glanced down at the hat, then at his heavy coat. 'You think they're over the top?'

'I didn't mean to criticize.'

'It was my wife's idea. Wear something Dickensian, she said. I rented them from a theatrical shop.'

At the door, he turned. The moonlight showed up his face, pale and sickly. My fire and mulled wine had clearly had no effect on him.

'People warned me off this house,' he said, chuckling wheezily. 'It's supposed to be haunted.'

'Really?'

'Yes. Have you ever seen or heard anything?'

'No.'

He nodded, satisfied, then gave a hacking cough and winced. 'I'd better be off. This fog catches my throat.' Settling the top-hat on his head, he stepped into the fog and was gone.

I went back to my fireside chair.

Haunted, indeed!

There are no ghosts in this house. I should know, if anyone does. I've never heard or seen one, and I've lived here for over three hundred years.

The Ghost of Christmas Shopping

Lesley Howarth

I'M a ghost, right? Haunting's my job. I get up and around, most years, about December the twenty-third. Or maybe the twenty-fourth. Call me lazy, but I never went much on getting up before I had to. There was a time, back when it's hard to remember, when I spent my *life* in bed. In hospital, that was. Then I got so I was OK to go home. Then I could go out shopping, so long as I didn't overdo it, or carry anything heavy. I left carrying things to Mum. I had to be careful a lot. I'm careful now. Catch me getting out of the freezer much before December the twenty-third, and you've got an exceptionally fine Christmas shopping frenzy.

I usually start flexing the old haunting muscles about the time most kids finally realize the chocolate in the advent calendar's the grisliest ever invented. Once the shoppers in the supermarket get that glazed look, when they'll buy just about *anything* with 'Festive Special' on it, that's about the time I stretch my legs. When they open up the freezer for those last-minute cocktail-size sausage rolls, that's my wake-up call. It's shopping fever that warms me up and sets me on my feet. Call me shallow, but I love that stuff. I suppose you could call me the ghost of Christmas shopping, except no one calls me anything. Ever. I did have another name, once.

Usually, I wake up in the frozen turkeys. Then I huff out when someone opens the freezer—you *can* have enough of frozen turkeys, know what I mean? Soon as I'm out of the freezer, I'm checking out trolleys for a likely family to hang out with over Christmas. A really classic trolley always grabs me.

So this year I'm cruising the aisles, right, and the trolleys are looking pretty mediocre, nothing too appealing—when I *actually spot the Stantons*. I almost *die*, except I did that already. See, I almost made it to lunch-time, last Christmas Day, with the Stantons. Except for Danny Stanton's puppy, I might be there now. The stuff with the puppy almost killed me all over again. *Look at him, isn't he great? What shall I call him? Rusty? Come on, Rusty. Thanks, Mum, thanks Dad. I really, really love him.*

Phew. Too much of that stuff, and I'm gone. Back in the freezer till next year. Love, generosity, Christmas spirit—it really turns me off. Call me freezer-fungus, only don't give me any of that heartwarming stuff. Maybe I *am* freezer-fungus, but I have to have something to feed off, you know. Even mould needs something to work with. I have to have hurt feelings, or at least a bit of rage. But Christmas spirit gets me. It makes me throw, it really does. I have to go back to my freezer. I don't have a lot of choice. It was too much to hope I'd make it through with the Stantons. Far too selfless, the Stantons. Pretty bleak Christmas all round.

So I've never yet made a whole Christmas day with *anyone*. So I'm thinking this year could be a first, and I'm chilling out on the corner between the deli and the Country Baker Mince Pie Offer, when I spot the perfect trolley. Very low fruit content, triple-choc super-soft ice-cream *plus* soft drinks so bright they bring on an additive high just *looking* at them. This is a trolley I can relate to. I tag along after the family. Mum, Dad, boy, girl. The little girl could be a problem. The little girl sees straight through me, and I know she's got me sussed.

'Kelly,' Mum asks her, 'wake up. What colour jelly d'you fancy?'

'Blackcurrant,' goes Kelly, staring hard. 'Tell him to go away.'

'Who?' says Mum. 'Lawrie?'

It looks like Lawrie's the brother. He's not much older than Kelly. He could be *younger* than Kelly, who knows? What am I, expert on children?

'Not *Lawrie*.' Old Kelly's going to blow it in a minute. I dredge up a smile, but she pulls Mum's coat and points. 'Not Lawrie,' she says, '*that* boy. Why's he following us?'

Mum looks round. 'What boy? Lawrie, get me a cheesecake mix. Down a bit. Left a bit. There.'

'Go *away*!' Kelly pouts. 'I don't *like* that boy.'

Phew. I make a face. It doesn't matter what I do. Mum's not really listening.

'Push the trolley,' says Mum, 'good girl. Let's get some biscuits, shall we? How about one of those selection tins with the pink wafers in it, would you like that?'

Lawrie drops a packet of cheesecake mix into the trolley. 'I want one of those chocolate things,' he says.

Lawrie points and he's right. I have to admit, the Festive Yule Log Offer's pretty tempting. Lawrie's mother agrees.

'We'll have a Yule Log as well,' she says. '*And* some frozen éclairs.'

Top shoppers, or what? I'm warming to this lot already. Dad wanders off to the Wines and Spirits. I trail the others round the freezers. They're real shopaholics, I'm glad to say. By the time we reach the checkout the trolley's landsliding twelve-pack crisps, ham, mallows, jelly, Father Christmas-shaped novelty bars, oven chips, party-poppers, crackers, Bumper Nut Assortments, Country Baker mince pies, ready-to-roll icing, instant trifle mix, cake, pudding, mini-rolls, Festive Flavour Corn Puffs, Yule Log, sausage rolls plus two fat selection stockings. And *that*'s just the stuff on top. Gross-out, or what? This is the family of my dreams.

I always *did* eat a lot. When I wasn't a ghost, I was fourteen. Then it was crisps, chips, biscuits, burgers, anything junky, OK? Now I'm a ghost, I feed on that special Christmas feeling of *never having enough* of whatever it was you really wanted. So you open all your presents, and the CD you got isn't right. The sweater someone bought you is *almost* right, except for the colour—are they *blind*? Plus your family's driving you mad. You wonder what Christmas is *for*, until Pictionary or Twister after dinner. Then the arguments start, and every other Christmas you ever remember comes flooding back with a bad taste, and instead of feeling sorry you feel spoiled and fed-up and ungrateful, like Christmas never gives you what you think it will, and somehow there must be more. That's what keeps me going. I always wanted *more*. Except every year, someone blows it. Sooner or later, someone does something nice or generous or heartwarming, and I'm gone. Can't stick that kind of thing.

Trolleys can tell you a lot. With a top trolley and no dates in sight— never bother haunting anyone with dates in their trolley, only sad people who never argue buy dates—the Bayleys make my day. I know they're called the Bayleys because I check out the cheque at the checkout. The squabble over the prawn crisps clinches it. The Battling Bayleys. I can feel it. I'm going to have a really joyful Christmas.

Kelly stuffs crisps and stares at me while her folks load up the car. You can get kids like this sometimes, the kind that's going to spot you right away. They tend to be a pain, except it doesn't matter too much what they say if they're little, because no one's going to believe they saw a ghost. Kelly's little. Six, maybe seven. I reckon it's a chance worth taking. I look back at the supermarket before we leave. *Ta-ra. Bye for now.* I've tried other stores, but you don't get the rush. Food shopping under pressure brings out the worst in people. I always come back to Super-Fare.

OK, Christmas Eve with the Bayleys rates eight on the aggro scale. Enough bad vibes to snack off, not enough to pig out. I rove around the house for a while, sampling this room, then that. The kitchen tastes good to me. Mum unpacks the Christmas cake. She takes out the ready-rolled icing and gets it all stuck to her hands. Finally, she gets it on the cake. It looks like a badly-fitting nappy. She pulls out the cake decorations and sticks on trees and a reindeer. The Father Christmas figure won't stand up. She screws him into the cake so he's up to his knees in Special Offer Marzipan. She's getting pretty cross.

I'm enjoying myself quite a bit, when Dad throws a wobbler in the loft: 'Where did that thingy with the brass cherubs on it go? You know. The thing you light candles on, and the cherubs go round and round? What? *I'm not getting a thing about it*. I'd just like to find it one year, that's all.'

Dad comes downstairs and ruins his suede shoes dribbling hot UHT cream out of a Country Baker mince pie onto 'em. The kids watch a Christmas Eve ghost story on the telly. I have to tell you, the ghost in the story's pretty weak. If you're talking technique, I could show it a thing or two. Some ghosts go in for traditional stuff like busting mirrors, rapping on walls, turning lights and taps on and off, that kind of thing. Not me. I usually go for something simple but classy, like bending every clock hand in the house, crossing knives on the table, spelling out letters on the floor with whatever comes in handy, swapping keys around, etc., etc. Switch on the telly in the middle of the night and throw in a nightmare for the family dog, plus a pool of tomato ketchup on the settee, and you got 'em thoroughly spooked.

Anyway, Christmas Eve around midnight, I slip into Kelly Bayley's room in reverse Father Christmas mode. Usually what I do is, I take all the kids' Christmas presents out of their sacks and distribute them in weird places. It always throws 'em on Christmas morning, when they wake up and find things upside down in the hall or undone all over the floor and they realize nobody did it. It freaks 'em out every time. I've never known it fail.

Kelly's hit the jackpot this year. This year her Christmas sack's *huge*. Her parents have bought up every tacky plastic toy there *is*, plus they've left her *two* confectionary stockings. In front of everything else is Candy's House. Kelly's main present is Candy's House. I unwrap its pink-and-purple chimney. Candy's House is all pink-and-purple, and so is Candy's Stable and Candy's Styles, the hairdresser's shop with *real* shower-heads for *real* styles. I know these things, you see. I see them on TV. Kelly also has Poppy Pinhole, the Pocket-Sized Doll That's Your Friend. I stuff Poppy Pinhole down the chimney of Candy's House, and move on before I hurl.

Moving on down the sack, I take out a couple more presents. One of them feels like a game, the other's a soft toy or something, so I drift out and leave it in the bath. I unwrap its head. It's a soft-toy Dalmatian puppy, cute or what? I leave it leering down the toilet with a shaving foam hat on its head. Then I drift into the kitchen and stick a few knives in the wall. It's not very nice, I know, but how else can I let them know I want less Christmas spirit, more aggro? Good thing the dog's in the garage. I know it knows I'm there.

So I shimmy back into the bedroom and ghost out a few more toys. It's quite exciting, you know? It makes me feel quite nostalgic. I had presents, once. Once I had a bike on Christmas morning. That was before I got ill. I think about what I was like before I got ill. Then I get out the Bumper Smarties from Kelly's confectionary stocking and spell out

G – R – A – N – T

in Smarties all over Kelly Bayley's bedroom floor, because Grant was my name when I had Christmases. I don't have Christmases now. Only the sparks off other people's. I could get sorry for myself.

To cheer myself up a bit, I put a few things in the fridge—a Bat Ball, an Etch-a-Sketch, and a pair of Glitter Leggings, and I hope they appreciate the joke. Back in the bedroom I spend quite a while balancing a board game over the door. Then just as I'm placing a Pocahontas Bubble Bath on the very *edge* of the bookcase, I hear a noise in the bed. I look around. She's watching me. Kelly Bayley's awake.

'Those aren't *your* presents,' she says. 'Father Christmas left them for *me*.'

Ghosts never panic, OK? They can speak to you if they want to, it's just that most of them don't.

'Leave my presents *alone*,' she says. 'They're not for you, they're for me.'

I know that—I'm just helping.

'No, you're not,' she says, 'you're hiding things, you are.'

No, I'm not.

'You are.'

I'm putting them in funny places.

'Well, you shouldn't. You should go home.'

If only. *Home*, I think.

'You don't have a home, do you?' Kelly Bayley sits up and gives me the stare. 'I know who you are,' she says. 'You're the supermarket ghost.'

So? I send her, crushingly. What does she want, a medal?

'You needn't think—'

Needn't think what?

'You needn't think you're spoiling Christmas—'

Who's spoiling Christmas?

'—cos I won't *let* you.' She rubs her eyes. She's tired. Good. With luck, I hope, in the morning, she won't remember a thing.

I never did nothing, all right? I only moved a few things.

'I can see what you're doing. It's mean.'

It's only a joke, OK?

'Well, why don't you just stop *doing* it? Why don't you just go away?'

I don't usually get this kind of thing. It's pretty upsetting, actually.

No one ever challenged me with those flashing brown eyes, the way Kelly Bayley does. With this kind of interference, the only thing to do is The Fade. I fade pretty quick, but is it *ever* a long time before she stops scouting the bedroom with those big brown eyes and finally goes back to sleep. By twelve forty-five I'm beginning to think the Bayleys may be my biggest mistake yet. I fade through the floor and rubbish the Christmas tree a bit, but it doesn't cheer me up as much as it usually does. For some reason.

> *'Tis the season to be jolly,*
> *Tra-la-la-la-la-la*
> *Tra-la-la-la*

Dad turns off the radio alarm. 'Happy Christmas, love.'

So it's Christmas morning and—BANG!—Kelly and Lawrie Bayley are *in* at their mum and dad's bedroom door and *all over* their mum and dad's bed with Christmas sacks and wrapping paper and tantrums, which is great, I mean, I'm *in*.

The first thing that happens is that Lawrie stands on his remote-control car. It's only his main present. He doesn't mean to. He didn't see it. He only just unwrapped it, and now it's *bro-oh-oh-ken*!

'And whose fault is that?' Dad says.

Lawrie's wail climbs higher and higher till Dad packs the car away and says he'll look at it later. He can look at it all he likes, it'll still be broken.

'It's broken an' *you* have to mend it!' Lawrie's spoilt tantrum explodes.

'I'll try to,' Dad says. 'Please.'

'An' you get your tool-box, please, an' you mend it *now*!'

'Lawrie,' Dad says, 'that will do.'

'Please. Can you. Mend it,' Lawrie huffs, through tears. 'Can you. Mend it. Now.'

'Not now, later,' Dad says. 'Open something else.'

'An'. You mend it. Now.'

He's really upset. I don't have to tell you, I'm enjoying myself. Lawrie's sending out these barb-shaped selfish feelings I can puff myself up with to make myself bigger, stronger. Dad's hurt feelings

give me back twice the energy I put out to make myself bigger. They don't even know they're doing it. It's a real Christmas breakfast. Enjoy.

Dad says, 'Shut *up*, Lawrie,' but Lawrie shuts up anyway, there's too many other things to open.

'COME-AN'-SEE-CANDY'S-HOUSE!' Kelly Bayley jumps up and runs in and out of her bedroom. Her mother follows her, laughing. 'AN'-HER-LIFT-GOES-UP-AN'-DOWN-IT-DOES-SO-CAN-YOU-COME-AN'-*SEE*?'

Kelly's mother sees. In the meantime, Lawrie's batteries don't fit his Super Stunt Racetrack. Dad nips downstairs to feed the dog, so Lawrie forces in the batteries anyway, but they really don't want to go. Before Dad pounds back upstairs, Lawrie's trashed his Racetrack. The cars will never race round like they should, and no one will ever know why.

Mum reappears with Kelly. Kelly's well over the top. She *loves* her slippers and Art Deck, her videos and Slime Monsterz game. Most of all, she loves Candy's House, except someone went in the chimney.

'Someone went in the chimney?' Dad looks pretty crummy. He looks like he just saw a ghost.

'They really did!' Kelly covers her mouth. She can hardly speak for giggling. She makes it the *funniest* thing. 'Someone put Poppy Pinhole down Candy's chimney,' she gets out at last, 'and I'm going to go and *get* her!'

Dad's white as a sheet since he went downstairs. He looks like a ghost himself. Now he turns to Kelly Bayley's mother. 'Helen—' he says.

'What?' she says. 'Hey,' she says. She looks at him. 'Hey, what's up with you?'

'Something's strange—I don't know.'

'What?' she says. 'What's strange?'

'I went downstairs to feed Nelson.' He takes a breath, and I know—don't you?—what's coming. 'I went downstairs to feed Nelson.' Another deep breath. 'And he wouldn't come into the kitchen. There's toys in the fridge, did you know? *And there's kitchen knives in the wall.*'

Kelly reappears in the doorway with Poppy Pinhole. 'Mum thinks

I must've got up in the night, but I didn't,' she tells Poppy Pinhole.

Kelly looks up. She's uncertain. She puts her head on one side.

'In my bedroom,' she says, 'why is there GRANT on the floor?'

I admit I've put them through it. I suppose you think I'm mean. I *am* mean, of course, that's the point. I'm not really dangerous, though, I'd just like to point out. Knives in the wall is as far as it goes with me. There *are* other ghosts I could mention—well, I could, but I won't.

So I make it through to dinner-time with the Bayleys. Almost half a Christmas day, it has to be some sort of record. Dinner's a real feast for me. I know I'm in for a treat when Lawrie looks at his sprouts.

'Eat up,' says Mum. 'It's only three sprouts. Think of all the people who haven't *got* any sprouts.'

Lawrie thinks. Then he says: 'An' *I* don't want any either.'

'What's that?' says Dad. 'Just you think about all the people who haven't got any Christmas dinners *at all*.'

Lawrie goes red. Then he jumps up and huffs off upstairs. I just *hoover* up the bruised feelings afterwards. That's what I *call* Christmas dinner.

Old Lawrie doesn't come downstairs again until quarter past two, by which time the pudding's well crusty. They *would* have to spoil everything and give him a cuddle. It's a dangerous moment, but it passes. Then they give him a choc-ice. Silly old sprouts, they say. Not worth getting upset about. Not on Christmas Day.

The afternoon's a bit so-so. A bit of aggro over telly schedules, nothing really tasty. Not that I mind after dinner. Dinner keeps me going until supper-time, no problem. By the time they're into the cold turkey sarnies, I don't mind admitting I'm a little peckish myself. I could do with a little resentment. I'm not fussy. A tiff would do, or an argument over a present—anything, really, to see me through till the Boxing Day niggles set in. I think I might be going to make it through a *whole Christmas Day* this time, I really do. All I need is a snack to keep me going. A scene before going to bed? That'll do nicely. Mum looks up at the clock once or twice, but Kelly Bayley ignores her. Bum in the air, she's playing a game. No one's put her to bed until now. She's done pretty well, keeping quiet.

Mum clears her throat. 'Kelly.'

I'm waiting to see what'll happen. There's got to be something in this for me. It could be just what I need.

'Look at the time.' Mum gets up. 'Kelly, did you hear me?'

Dad says, 'Come on, Kelly, time for bed.'

Kelly frowns. 'Can't I stay up? *Please?*'

'You *have* stayed up. It's nine o'clock. Enough excitement for one day.'

'But I just want to do my Zoo Quiz one more time. Just only one more—'

'Kelly.' Dad looks up.

Kelly Bayley opens her mouth. She's about to make a scene. Then she looks at me. She looks at me, and she *knows.*

Then you know what she does? Instead of stamping and crying and flushing and sending out sparks I can use, she does *completely the reverse.* Kelly Bayley looks at me the way she looked at me in her bedroom the night before Christmas. Then she goes up to Mum in her stupid panda slippers and her dumb-looking glitter wig and her brand-new Christmas nightdress, and you know what she says?

She says, 'Thanks for Christmas Day, Mum. It was *brilliant.*'

'Well, it's been a funny old Christmas Day.'

I'll say. They only searched the house from top to bottom, Mum and Dad, and then they put away all the knives and anything else sharp you could cut with. At least it brought them together at Christmas time. That's the way I look at it, anyway.

'Thanks for all my presents,' Kelly Bayley says, 'and for everything else, *ever.* You're my *best* Mum and Dad.'

You're my *best* Mum and Dad. Can you believe that? Thanks for Christmas Day, Mum. It was *brilliant.* And old Kelly Bayley, she kisses her mother goodnight. And Mum hugs her tight, eyes closed, folding her warm in her arms. And—thanks, Kelly Bayley—I'm gone.

Families. It happens every year. Sooner or later, they get to you with some gen-u-ine love and warmth. There's no stopping them. What would a Christmas without warmth be? It'd be, well—cold. Like me. Pretty soon now I'll be climbing back into my freezer. Soon I'll be frozen stiff, well out of it till next year's happy shoppers come to warm me up. It doesn't usually bother me. But this year, I think it might.

Right now, the supermarket's dead. All the aisles are cold and dark and empty. The plastic strip-curtain by the deli counter clacks a bit in the draught. The checkouts loom at the far end like the keys of some piano no one plays any more. I picture the once-feverish Christmas shoppers, home now with Grade A headaches and a nagging feeling that the guarantee for the joystick someone stood on went out in the bin with the wrapping paper. Christmas. Why can't it be simple?

I wouldn't mind, but they never learn. They'll do it again, just the same, next year. The last week before Christmas they'll be back in their droves in panic mode, scrabbling for frozen turkeys in my freezer, waking me up, as usual, when shopping fever peaks. I start wondering about them all, hoping everyone got what they really deserved this Christmas. Then I pull myself up. What am I, the Christmas fairy?

I count cut-price offers for a while. Then I start thinking about Kelly Bayley. I wish I could stop, but I can't. *You needn't think you're spoiling Christmas*, she says. *It's mean*, she says. *Why don't you just stop doing it?* And her brown eyes scout me up and down.

Maybe she's right. Maybe I *should* stop doing it. Why be a mean ghost when I could be the Ghost of Family Feeling? The Ghost of Icky Moments? The Ghost of Going-To-Bed-Nicely? Right now, I'm thinking maybe a change of diet next Christmas mightn't be so bad. I may just try chewing on a little goodwill-to-all, why not? Not as good as ice-cream. But probably better than sour grapes, whatever *they* taste like. I picture Kelly Bayley snuggling down in bed, glitter wig stowed on the lamp-stand so she spots it first thing in the morning. I picture her waking up, clapping it on, rushing downstairs in her dressing-gown for Boxing Day cartoons. Hey, Kelly Bayley, you've got me thinking I've changed. No kidding. Can I come Christmas Day next year? See you in your brand-new smartypants outfit? With your next year's novelty slippers snapping on your feet? And stick around till midnight, even, like I never did before? Would you let me, Kelly Bayley? I promise I wouldn't eat too much. I'd do anything you tell me.

So, that's about it for this year. Nothing lonelier than a supermarket at midnight on the twenty-fifth of December, so I might as well pack up right now. The freezer sighs as I open the lid. *My* freezer. The freezer I was looking in when I haemorrhaged. When I was fourteen. When I was Christmas shopping. With Mum. I died on the way to hospital. But I found my way back straight away. Been hanging around ever since. The Ghost of Christmas Shopping. I tell you, it almost frightens *me*.

Not Wanting the Blue Cracker

Dennis Hamley

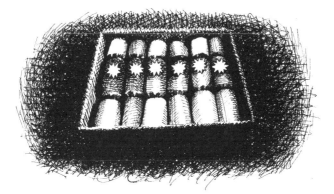

K ERRY and her mother surveyed the Christmas lunch table they
had laid between them.

'It's a real work of art,' said Mum.

Kerry agreed. It was indeed, from the rarely-seen creamy-white
lace-embroidered tablecloth to the scented candles flickering in the
candelabra placed in the middle.

'I love the way you've done the serviettes,' said Mum.

Kerry had taken the red paper serviettes with holly leaves printed
round the edges and made them into little pyramids which she had
placed on each side plate. It was nice to be given such a compliment.
'Thank you,' she said.

The silver cutlery which only came out of its box for very special
occasions shone softly: the seldom-used lead glass goblets for the
grown-ups' wine flashed like icy stars. Perhaps, Kerry thought, on
this day of kindness, compliments, and indulgence there might be a
sip of Chardonnay for her too—though if there were, it would be from
a wine glass from the kitchen. After all, there were six goblets and six
grown-ups to drink out of them: Mum and Dad, elder sister Margie
and husband Jeff, elder brother Ray and his wife Gloria.

Six grown-ups and six kids. Kerry sniffed as she reluctantly put herself in that category even though she was twelve—an afterthought appearing to everyone's surprise when Ray was sixteen and Margie eighteen. There was no argument about whether the others were kids or not. Margie and Jeff had three children, eight-year-old twins Melanie and Brian and Michelle, five. Ray and Gloria had two boys, Jamie, seven, and Jack, three.

At the moment they were all in the sitting room with the Christmas tree. Brian was watching Jamie on his new Playstation and Melanie was folding used wrapping paper into neat squares. Kerry had been called in to quieten Jack when he thought he'd broken his new Thomas the Tank Engine. She had demonstrated there was nothing wrong with Thomas by fiddling with him and then making him go. Even so, Michelle had run to where Margie and Gloria downed bacardis and Coke and Kerry's dad, Ray and Jeff did the same with cans of lager. 'Auntie Gloria, Kerry's breaking Jack's new Thomas the Tank Engine,' she shouted. Dad and Jeff were at once despatched to sort it out. They poked around poor Thomas's insides, mucked him up again and Jamie howled afresh. After that, helping Mum lay the table was like heaven.

Now it was time to set out the greatest glory in the dining room. *Crackers.*

Yes, there were some cheap supermarket crackers left from last year in the cupboard under the stairs. But Mum had said, 'Let's treat ourselves now we've got the whole family coming for Christmas.' She'd taken Kerry into the most exclusive shop in town where they had bought a box of twelve incredibly expensive crackers containing, they were assured, gifts really worth having. Six were a deep wine-red, six a lovely midnight blue. On the red crackers were intricate designs chased in gold: on the blue crackers, the designs were in silver. It seemed a crime to pull them.

Seeing the crackers had given Kerry an idea. She had dragged Mum to an art shop, where she bought red and blue card, a little tin of gold paint and another of silver, and a tiny, fine paint brush.

'I'll set the crackers out red, blue, red, blue all the way round the table and make name tags to match so everyone knows where they're sitting,' said Kerry.

'I'll show you how I want the seating arranged,' said Mum.

When they were home, Kerry cut out the tags and painted the names, gold on red and silver on blue. Dad, sitting at the head of the table, had a red cracker and red name tag. Margie next to him on his left had blue. Then came Michelle next to her with red, then Ray, blue. After that it was Melanie, red; Kerry, blue; then, at the other end of the table and conveniently close to the kitchen, Mum, red. Up the other side were, next to Mum, Jamie, blue; Jeff, red; Brian, blue; Gloria, red—and last of all, three-year-old Jack, blue. This was Jack's first Christmas out of his high chair, so he was next to his mother. On the other side sat Dad, who'd been saying, 'He may be a big boy like the rest but he still needs his old grandad to keep an eye on him.'

As she laid the crackers out with their matching name tags, Kerry had a very faint qualm of foreboding. 'Mum, why are we all sitting mixed up like this?' she said.

Mum, adjusting the position of a wine glass on its coaster, said nothing.

'Did you hear me, Mum?'

Mum turned to her, a harassed look on her face. 'Yes, I heard you, love,' she said. 'If you must know, it's because Christmas is a funny old time of the year. It shouldn't be but it is.'

'What do you mean?'

'Things always seem to go wrong at Christmas. If I put the grown-ups together and all you kids—' Kerry winced—'separately, the grown-ups would forget about the kids and the kids would start terrible fights and you, poor Kerry, would end up having to sort them out. But if I put the families together, so Ray's lot face Margie's lot, then as soon as there's a few drinks down them, they'll argue and shout at each other and there's no end to the disaster there'd be. Your father would join in on Margie's side because you girls have always been his favourites and I'd come in on Ray's side out of fairness. Nobody would speak to each other until Easter, your father and me included. No, this is the best way—split them up. Divide and rule. Though Gloria has to sit next to little Jack because he may need some help with the turkey and I wouldn't trust your father to be any good with him.'

By now the whole house was full of the smell of roasted turkey and Kerry was hungry. 'Isn't it ready yet, Mum?' she said.

Mum seemed suddenly to remember her half-consumed glass of sherry and gulped it down. 'I hope so,' she replied. The laughter in the sitting room was getting louder. 'They're in a right state already in there. They must be on the whisky.'

The turkey and chestnut stuffing were cooked and so were the vegetables. Mum called out, 'Eddie, are you going to carve?' Dad couldn't have heard her: his voice crowed, 'Guess what he said next,' and a gale of laughter showed it might be some time before anyone found out.

Mum sniffed. 'If you want anything done, do it yourself,' she said and set to with the carving knife. Meanwhile, Kerry took dishes full of vegetables and set them on the table. Then she fetched plates with ready-carved turkey on them, set out to Mum's instructions. 'A leg for your dad and one for Ray. Jeff has the biggest of the other plates. These are for Margie and Gloria, these little ones for the kids. Tell me how much you want, Kerry.' Then she shouted into the dining room, 'Eddie, if you wouldn't carve the turkey, at least open the wine.'

This time Dad heard, came into the kitchen, seized the corkscrew and opened a bottle of French white and another of Australian red.

'You should have opened the red earlier to let it breathe,' said Mum.

'Ah, what does it matter? They won't notice,' said Dad and strode off into the dining room with them, shouting, 'Plenty more where these came from.' His voice made Kerry wonder how many cans of lager and glasses of whisky were sloshing round in that capacious stomach.

'Come on, everybody, stir yourselves,' cried Mum. 'The turkey's on the table and getting cold with waiting for you.'

Everybody walked slightly shamefacedly into the dining room. They filed round the table looking for their places as reverently as if they were in church. When they had found them, they stood behind their chairs as if not knowing quite what to do next.

'Sit down, everyone,' said Mum. Everyone did except Gloria, who sat as soon as she had helped Jack into his chair next to her. 'What a beautiful table,' she said.

'Thank you,' said Mum. 'But most of it is Kerry's doing.'

'Oh, Kerry,' said Margie. 'Did you make these little pyramids out of the serviettes?'

'Yes,' Kerry answered. Another compliment coming?

'They're lovely. I wish I could do them. They just crumple up when I try.' She looked further round the table. 'And look at the beautiful crackers. Did you set them out like this, Kerry—red, blue, red, blue, with the matching name tags? That's really clever.'

'Yes, I did,' said Kerry.

There was a murmur of approbation about everything that Kerry had done to make the table such a wonderful sight.

Then three-year-old Jack said, 'Don't want a blue cracker.'

'That's all right, little man,' said Gloria. 'I'll have your blue one and you can have Mummy's red one.' She changed them over. 'There, that's settled,' she said. Jack surveyed the red cracker critically, then put it to one side.

'No, it's not settled,' said Margie to her sister-in-law. 'You've spoilt the arrangement. You've ruined Kerry's lovely table.'

There was sudden quiet all round the table. Then Mum said, 'Dig in to the vegetables everybody,' in an unnaturally bright-sounding voice. But nobody did. They waited for Gloria's answer.

It soon came. 'It's none of your business what I do with my children.' Gloria's face had turned an ominous pink.

'I won't have that,' Margie burst out. 'It isn't fair on poor Kerry. She spent hours setting the table the way she wanted and it's not right some little snotty-nose spoils it for her. He shouldn't get his own way.'

'It doesn't matter, Margie,' said Kerry.

'Yes, it *does* matter,' said Margie hotly. 'You worked hard on this.'

'Don't you dare tell me what to do with my own son, Margie,' Gloria shouted.

'You spoil him,' Margie replied. 'You spoil his brother Jamie as well.' Her face, as opposed to Gloria's pinkness, was going pale with fury. As if stung by the accusation, Jack burst into tears.

'Now look what you've done,' said Gloria. 'I'd rather spoil them than have three deprived kids like yours. You never go anywhere with them, you never give them anything nice. Poor Brian and Melanie.

Not to mention little Michelle. I've watched them today, bored out of their minds by the cheapskate presents you've given them.'

'*Cheapskate?*' Margie looked ready to reach across Dad and hit Gloria.

'Yes, cheapskate. Seeing the way you bring those three up told me what I shouldn't do when I had mine.'

'Quiet, Gloria,' muttered Ray. 'Give it a rest, for God's sake. It's Christmas.'

'I don't care when it is. She's not talking to me like that.'

But nothing would stop Margie now. 'Kids have got to learn it's a hard world out there. You're making a rod for your own back, giving Jamie and Jack everything they want. One day you'll be very sorry.'

'Don't you tell me how to bring my kids up.'

'And don't you insult me over mine.'

'Please, stop it, both of you,' Mum pleaded. But they didn't listen.

'Just keep your mouth shut, Margie,' Gloria yelled. 'You always spoil everything.'

'*I* spoil everything?' Margie could hardly get the words out for rage. 'That's rich, coming from you.'

She turned to Jeff, who was looking at the tablecloth as if deciphering secret messages in the embroidery. 'Are you going to let her get away with that?' she cried. 'Say something, for heaven's sake.'

'What do you want me to say?' Jeff asked mildly.

'Tell Ray to make his wife button her lip.'

'Excuse me, Ray . . .' Jeff began, but Margie and Gloria together interrupted him. Margie shouted, 'Oh, you're useless,' to Jeff while Gloria looked straight at Ray and shouted, 'See what I mean about them? They're all the same, your family.'

Dad heard that and, as Mum had predicted to Kerry, weighed in on Margie's side. 'Have you been talking about us behind our backs?'

There was a short silence, though long enough for Jamie to say, 'Mum, if you're going to be arguing again, can I go back to my Playstation?'

'No, you can *not*,' Gloria answered.

Margie now addressed her husband Jeff triumphantly. 'There you are. I was right. She doesn't worry about what she says in front of her children. God knows what those poor creatures have to put up with.'

'Eat up, everybody. The turkey will go cold,' said Mum, trying to sound bright and failing.

It seemed Gloria would rather go hungry. She was screaming at Margie. 'Now who's been talking behind people's backs?' She turned to Mum. 'Oh, this proves it, doesn't it. You never liked me in this family, since the day your Ray first brought me round here. Well, I know when I'm not wanted.'

'There's no need for that, love,' said Ray.

'Don't you "love" me, Ray,' she answered. 'We're going. Come on.' She stood up dramatically. 'Jamie, get up out of that chair and get ready.'

'What about my Playstation?'

'Oh, shut up about your precious Playstation. We're going,' Gloria snapped, pulling Jack out of his chair.

Now Dad stood up as well, swaying slightly. 'If you go out of this house, you never come here again.'

'Suits us,' said Gloria. 'Doesn't it, Ray?'

Ray sat still, said nothing and looked miserable. Gloria bent down and yelled in his ear. 'Are you staying here? Because if so, you'll find the door locked when you come home.'

Unwillingly, Ray rose to his feet.

Now Kerry stood as well. She saw all the angry people. She saw the children shocked into silence. She saw her mother sitting next to her, tears streaming down her face. She knew that in two more seconds Gloria and Ray would be gone, Jamie and Jack with them, and not only Christmas but family life would be ruined for ever. And she drew on every ounce of resolution that she had and shouted, 'SIT DOWN, THE LOT OF YOU!'

The shock filled the room like electricity and made them all stop in their tracks. Mum dried her tears and looked at her daughter, stunned. Ray sat down. Gloria didn't, but at least she didn't go any further.

'SIT DOWN!' Kerry cried again. This time, even Gloria did. Everyone looked at Kerry, as if expecting something more.

Suddenly, she knew what it was. 'Wait,' she said. 'Don't move.'

She went into the hall and the cupboard under the stairs where the Christmas decorations were kept. She scrabbled around in the dark until she found the cheap supermarket crackers left over from the previous year. She pulled the box out, came back to the dining room and showed it to Jack, whose crying had dwindled into occasional snuffles.

'Look,' she said. 'Green ones.'

Jack poked at them suspiciously. Then he took one out, a broad smile on his face. 'I like green crackers,' he said. Kerry held the box out and he grabbed at two more. 'Want lots of green crackers,' he said. Soon he was surrounded by, nearly buried in, green crackers. Suddenly he was happy, and his happiness spread round the table, together with huge relief, until the air almost sang with them.

Gloria and Margie looked at each other, embarrassed. Then Margie said, 'Sorry, Gloria.'

'No,' said Gloria. 'It was my fault, not yours. I shouldn't have flown off the handle like that. Your presents aren't really cheapskate.'

'Yours aren't too extravagant,' said Margie. They left their chairs, met, embraced, kissed and came back smiling.

'If anybody's meal has gone cold, I'll put it in the microwave for a couple of minutes to heat it up,' said Mum. Then: 'Eddie, you never poured the wine.'

'No more I did,' said Dad. 'Who's for red, who's for white?' When he had finished going round the table, he said, 'Have all the kids got cans of Coke?' Then he said to Kerry, 'Get yourself a glass from the kitchen, love. You deserve a drop.'

So Kerry did, and when Dad had filled it with white wine he said, 'Is everybody ready? Let's drink a toast.'

So they all, grown-ups and kids, raised their glasses or their cans and Dad said, 'Well, after that silly fuss, let's drink to us all and may we never forget how thankful and happy we ought to be. So let's have a really merry Christmas,' and they all answered, 'Merry Christmas.'

And then Jack said, 'Want a blue cracker.'

The Nativity Bell and the Falconer

George Mackay Brown

FERGUS and the seven brothers who were left stood in the door of the little monastery of St Peter. The seamen from the east had put great wounds upon it, three Easters since. Many windows were broken. The fires had lapped the walls of refectory and dormitory and had broken through those roofs; the tapestry was torn from the chapel wall; the statues of the Queen of Heaven and St Peter were overset and scored with axe-gashes; chalice and candlesticks stolen. But the chapel roof was intact. The bell hung in the belfry still, a heavy flower.

Father Fergus had rowed across from Eynhallow island at dawn. Their little ox-hide boat lay high on the beach, safe from the pealing waves.

A seal watched from far out on a skerry.

Their curragh had been seen out in the sound, crossing over. Singly, and in small groups, the islanders now came slowly towards the monastery.

'Who knows?' said Fergus. 'They may be glad to see us. It is midwinter, Yule. They may want us to go away at once. Our little

Celtic communities always drew the longships. We excite the viking greed. Our silence irritates them.'

The islanders approached slowly. They were both glad and afraid.

'Oh,' said the oldest man, 'what would we do now in midwinter, at the year's death, without your bell and your psalms, and your story of the birth in the cowshed?'

'You'll have them,' said Fergus. 'Tonight at midnight is the time. Darkness and winter and death will be put to flight. We will celebrate the Nativity here once more.'

The islanders were glad. Silent joy passed from face to face. Even the face of the youngest child, carried by his mother, smiled.

'It isn't possible, Father,' said the old man. 'I must tell you this, the Norsemen are in the island now. Surely you have heard it, in the other monastery in Eynhallow where you have been since you were driven out, that terrible plough-time? A longship came a week ago. There was no harrying and burning and going away again. They have taken over the big farm at the east shore of the island. That was my farm before the burning. They carried up ploughs from the ship. You can't see the ship from here, it is drawn up on the beach below the big farm. They have patched the roof of the farmhouse with clean Norwegian wood. We see smoke from the farm every night. We hear their shouts. We keep well to this side of the hill.'

'We will stay for this night,' said Fergus. 'We will celebrate the Feast of the Nativity. Perhaps we'll stay all the twelve days till the Feast of Epiphany.'

'I must tell you this,' said the old farmer. 'They have their axes too. Their longship has the dragon on it, breathing blood and flames. They have a man watching every day from the hilltop there. They know you and the brothers are here. Go now, before they sharpen the blades and light the torches.'

'Yes,' said a young man. 'It is great joy for us to have you here at midwinter. But there is too much danger.'

'They are a terrible people,' said the old man. 'One of them has lured the hawk out of the cloud and put a hood on it. The hawk hunts for them.'

'You are welcome to the Mass at midnight,' said Father Fergus. 'We have brought another chalice. The candles will burn in new tall silver.'

The old man turned, shaking his head. The islanders followed, singly or in groups, to their huts on the barren side of the hill.

The light was brief, between dawn and sunset. The Celtic monks set the chapel in order. They stretched sewn skins over the charred dormitory beams. It would be possible to sleep, if the weather continued mild and bright.

'What fools we are!' cried Brother Cormac. 'We have brought fuel but we have left the food and drink in Rousay.'

'Light the fire,' said Fergus. 'It will be a cold night. A fast won't hurt us.'

At noon the brothers saw a young bright-haired man, a stranger, down at the shore. He was speaking to the seal. The seal turned huge questing eyes on the man from the dragon-ship. It lifted its head.

At sunset the little community chanted the prayers and psalms in the hacked and burnt chapel.

They had set up the statues in their places, The Star of the Sea and The Fisherman.

The candles scooped shadows on their bent faces. The candles put a wavering brightness on their lifted psalming faces.

They trooped out of the chapel, slowly, one after the other.

They saw, against the sunset, on the hilltop, a single figure, watching.

'Oh,' said the youngest brother, beside the fire, 'I am hungry. We are all hungry.'

'There are people hungrier than us,' said Fergus. 'Everywhere. Always. The innkeeper is turning the man and the woman away. *No, he is saying, I am full up. There's nothing for you . . .*'

The boy wanted to say also that he was afraid. But Fergus, in that case, would say that fear was universal, but it could be overcome by love.

The boy started. There was a splash and a commotion at the shore below. 'It is the seal,' said the monk who stood at the door, keeping watch. 'All nature is full of the expectation of great joy.'

At Evensong, a few of the crofters and fishermen came in and knelt at the back of the chapel.

The candles burned like stars: pure cold flames.

The plainchant filled the chapel with such beauty that the old man whose farm had been taken, wept.

He said to Father Fergus in the chapel door, 'There's silence on the far side of the hill, in the farm. I am uneasy always when those men are silent.'

'Bring all the people at midnight,' said Fergus. 'It will be a joyful feast. You can bring your ox too and leave it at the door. The Feast is for all creation.'

It was a still evening. They could hear the seal plashing in the shallows.

'Don't ring the bell,' said the old man. 'That maddens them. They light the torches. They sharpen their axes then.'

The tongue of the bell kissed the rim, once, under the arch of the stars, and circle after circle of sound went wavering over the island.

The boy pulled the rope, and the bell cried, and sent out richer circles of sound.

The bell nodded and cried in a regular rhythm, it pealed, it sent out joyful surge upon surge.

At the altar, Fergus lit the candles.

He turned and climbed the stone spiral to the bell-ringer. 'Well done,' he said. 'You made a good sound. You must come now and serve me at the altar.'

Outside in the darkness were stumblings and cries, a lowing and a whinny or two. Shadows loomed out of darkness. It was the Pictish folk, all thirty of them, from the elder with the harsh grey beard to a swaddled infant on its mother's back. And more than them. They were leading and driving the three oxen and the dozen goats. The fishermen carried their oars and lines. The youngest fisherman brought a gift of haddocks. The young mother presented goat cheeses. The doorkeeper accepted them at the door.

Some of the people were looking fearfully behind them, from time to time, into the darkness.

The great broken net of stars reached from horizon to horizon.

The night was very still, after the bell-summons. Then they heard the plash below, off the skerry.

'The seal isn't asleep either,' said the boy.

'Come into the chapel,' said Fergus to the folk. 'The unborn King will be pleased with your gifts. The animals will have to remain outside. The wonder will be for them too.'

The Celtic monks were already in their places in the choir, kneeling. Candle-light laved their bald bowed heads and clasped hands.

The thirty islanders knelt and crossed themselves (the crosses like shields in front of them, for defence).

Fergus and the young monk came and stood at the altar, with bread and wine and book, between the candles.

The Mass of the Nativity was about to begin.

The latch lifted. A star-cold air entered the chapel and the candle flames fluttered and then were still again.

A stranger with wings of bronze-gold hair about his shoulders, and a bronze beard, came in. He turned and beckoned. Other young men followed him: seven.

A stir of terror went though the islanders. They made raggedly, shields and crosses in the air, to defend them. 'The first one to come in,' whispered the old Pict, 'is the one who took the hawk from the cloud and put the hood on it.'

At the altar the priest read the opening psalms. The boy's hand, turning the page, trembled. The kneeling monks did not look round.

. . . Filius mens es tu, ego hodie genui te. Quare fremuerunt gentes: et populi meditate sunt inania? Gloria . . .

Two of the Norsemen were carrying awkward burdens. They set them against the scorched wall of the chapel.

Then all seven of the Norsemen came and knelt, one after the other, on the cold stones, between the islanders and the monks in the choir.

Outside, under the silver star-web, the ox bellowed once. A goat snickered.

The young monk looked once towards the corner of the chapel where the men from the dragon-ship had set down their burdens. A scattering of barley had fallen from the sack and lay about the floor. The great jar was full of mead—there was no mistaking the honey smell, the essence of last summer's bee-labour in the east, in a Norwegian flower-starred valley . . .

—*Dominus vobiscum*

—*Et cum spiritu tuo*

The islanders saw that the falconer, kneeling on the cold stone, had brought his hands together, and they seemed to make in the air the shape of a dove, furled.

The Star
Arthur C. Clarke

IT is three thousand light-years to the Vatican. Once, I believed that space could have no power over faith, just as I believed that the heavens declared the glory of God's handiwork. Now I have seen that handiwork, and my faith is sorely troubled. I stare at the crucifix that hangs on the cabin wall above the Mark VI Computer, and for the first time in my life I wonder if it is no more than an empty symbol.

I have told no one yet, but the truth cannot be concealed. The facts are there for all to read, recorded on the countless miles of magnetic tape and the thousands of photographs we are carrying back to Earth. Other scientists can interpret them as easily as I can, and I am not one who would condone that tampering with the truth which often gave my order a bad name in the olden days.

The crew are already sufficiently depressed: I wonder how they will take this ultimate irony. Few of them have any religious faith, yet they will not relish using this final weapon in their campaign against me—that private, good-natured, but fundamentally serious, war which lasted all the way from Earth. It amused them to have a Jesuit as chief astrophysicist: Dr Chandler, for instance, could never get over it (why are medical men such notorious atheists?). Sometimes he would meet me on the observation deck, where the lights are always low so that the stars shine with undiminished glory. He would come up to me in the gloom and stand staring out of the great oval port, while the heavens crawled slowly around us as the ship turned end over end with the residual spin we had never bothered to correct.

'Well, Father,' he would say at last, 'it goes on forever and forever, and perhaps *Something* made it. But how you can believe that Something has a special interest in us and our miserable little world—that just beats me.' Then the argument would start, while the stars and nebulae would swing around us in silent, endless arcs beyond the flawlessly clear plastic of the observation port.

It was, I think, the apparent incongruity of my position that caused most amusement to the crew. In vain I would point to my three papers in the *Astrophysical Journal*, my five in the *Monthly Notices of the Royal Astronomical Society*. I would remind them that my order has long been famous for its scientific works. We may be few now, but ever since the eighteenth century we have made contributions to astronomy and geophysics out of all proportion to our numbers. Will my report on the Phoenix Nebula end our thousand years of history? It will end, I fear, much more than that.

I do not know who gave the nebula its name, which seems to me a very bad one. If it contains a prophecy, it is one that cannot be verified for several billion years. Even the word nebula is misleading: this is a far smaller object than those stupendous clouds of mist—the stuff of unborn stars—that are scattered throughout the length of the Milky Way. On the cosmic scale, indeed, the Phoenix Nebula is a tiny thing—a tenuous shell of gas surrounding a single star.

Or what is left of a star . . .

The Rubens engraving of Loyola seems to mock me as it hangs there above the spectrophotometer tracings. What would *you*, Father, have made of this knowledge that has come into my keeping, so far from the little world that was all the universe you knew? Would your faith have risen to the challenge, as mine has failed to do?

You gaze into the distance, Father, but I have travelled a distance beyond any that you could have imagined when you founded our order a thousand years ago. No other survey ship has been so far from

Earth: we are at the very frontiers of the explored universe. We set out to reach the Phoenix Nebula, we succeeded, and we are homeward bound with our burden of knowledge. I wish I could lift that burden from my shoulders, but I call to you in vain across the centuries and the light-years that lie between us.

On the book you are holding the words are plain to read. AD MAIOREM DEI GLORIAM, the message runs, but it is a message I can no longer believe. Would you still believe it, if you could see what we have found?

We knew, of course, what the Phoenix Nebula was. Every year, in our galaxy alone, more than a hundred stars explode, blazing for a few hours or days with thousands of times their normal brilliance before they sink back into death and obscurity. Such are the ordinary novae—the commonplace disasters of the universe. I have recorded the spectrograms and light curves of dozens since I started working at the Lunar Observatory.

But three or four times in every thousand years occurs something beside which even a nova pales into total insignificance.

When a star becomes a *supernova*, it may for a little while outshine all the massed suns of the galaxy. The Chinese astronomers watched this happen in AD 1054, not knowing what it was they saw. Five centuries later, in 1572, a supernova blazed in Cassiopeia so brilliantly that it was visible in the daylight sky. There have been three more in the thousand years that have passed since then.

Our mission was to visit the remnants of such a catastrophe, to reconstruct the events that led up to it, and, if possible, to learn its cause. We came slowly in through the concentric shells of gas that had been blasted out six thousand years before, yet were expanding still. They were immensely hot, radiating even now with a fierce violet light, but were far too tenuous to do us any damage. When the star had exploded, its outer layers had been driven upward with such speed that they had escaped completely from its gravitational field. Now they formed a hollow shell large enough to engulf a thousand solar systems, and at its centre burned the tiny, fantastic object which the star had now become—a White Dwarf, smaller than the Earth, yet weighing a million times as much.

The glowing gas shells were all around us, banishing the normal night of interstellar space. We were flying into the centre of a cosmic bomb that had detonated millennia ago and whose incandescent fragments were still hurtling apart. The immense scale of the explosion, and the fact that the debris already covered a volume of space many billions of miles across, robbed the scene of any visible movement. It would take decades before the unaided eye could detect any motion in these tortured wisps and eddies of gas, yet the sense of turbulent expansion was overwhelming.

We had checked our primary drive hours before, and were drifting slowly towards the fierce little star ahead. Once it had been a sun like our own, but it had squandered in a few hours the energy that should have kept it shining for a million years. Now it was a shrunken miser, hoarding its resources as if trying to make amends for its prodigal youth.

No one seriously expected to find planets. If there had been any before the explosion, they would have been boiled into puffs of vapour, and their substance lost in the greater wreckage of the star itself. But we made the automatic search, as we always do when approaching an unknown sun, and presently we found a single small world circling the star at an immense distance. It must have been the Pluto of this vanished solar system, orbiting on the frontiers of the night. Too far from the central sun ever to have known life, its remoteness had saved it from the fate of all its lost companions.

The passing fires had seared its rocks and burned away the mantle of frozen gas that must have covered it in the days before the disaster. We landed, and we found the Vault.

Its builders had made sure that we should. The monolithic marker that stood above the entrance was now a fused stump, but even the first long-range photographs told us that here was the work of intelligence. A little later we detected the continent-wide pattern of radioactivity that had been buried in the rock. Even if the pylon above the Vault had been destroyed, this would have remained, an immovable and all but eternal beacon calling to the stars. Our ship fell towards this gigantic bull's-eye like an arrow into its target.

The pylon must have been a mile high when it was built, but now it

looked like a candle that had melted down into a puddle of wax. It took us a week to drill through the fused rock, since we did not have the proper tools for a task like this. We were astronomers, not archaeologists, but we could improvise. Our original purpose was forgotten: this lonely monument, reared with such labour at the greatest possible distance from the doomed sun, could have only one meaning. A civilization that knew it was about to die had made its last bid for immortality.

It will take us generations to examine all the treasures that were placed in the Vault. They had plenty of time to prepare, for their sun must have given its first warnings many years before the final detonation. Everything that they wished to preserve, all the fruit of their genius, they brought here to this distant world in the days before the end, hoping that some other race would find it and that they would not be utterly forgotten. Would we have done as well, or would we have been too lost in our own misery to give thought to a future we could never see or share?

If only they had had a little more time! They could travel freely enough between the planets of their own sun, but they had not yet learned to cross the interstellar gulfs, and the nearest solar system was a hundred light-years away. Yet even had they possessed the secret of the Transfinite Drive, no more than a few millions could have been saved. Perhaps it was better thus.

Even if they had not been so disturbingly human as their sculpture shows, we could not have helped admiring them and grieving for their fate. They left thousands of visual records and the machines for projecting them, together with elaborate pictorial instructions from which it will not be difficult to learn their written language. We have examined many of these records, and brought to life for the first time in six thousand years the warmth and beauty of a civilization that in many ways must have been superior to our own. Perhaps they only showed us the best, and one can hardly blame them. But their worlds were very lovely, and their cities were built with a grace that matches anything of man's. We have watched them at work and play, and listened to their musical speech sounding across the centuries. One scene is still before my eyes—a group of children on a beach of strange blue sand, playing in the waves as children play on Earth. Curious whiplike trees line the shore, and some very large animal is wading in the shallows yet attracting no attention at all.

And sinking into the sea, still warm and friendly and life-giving, is the sun that will soon turn traitor and obliterate all this innocent happiness.

Perhaps if we had not been so far from home and so vulnerable to loneliness, we should not have been so deeply moved. Many of us had seen the ruins of ancient civilizations on other worlds, but they had never affected us so profoundly. This tragedy was unique. It is one thing for a race to fail and die, as nations and cultures have done on Earth. But to be destroyed so completely in the full flower of its achievement, leaving no survivors—how could that be reconciled with the mercy of God?

My colleagues have asked me that, and I have given what answers I can. Perhaps you could have done better, Father Loyola, but I have found nothing in the *Exercitia Spiritualia* that helps me here. They were not an evil people: I do not know what gods they worshipped, if indeed they worshipped any. But I have looked back at them across the centuries, and have watched while the loveliness they used their last strength to preserve was brought forth again into the light of their shrunken sun. They could have taught us much: why were they destroyed?

I know the answers that my colleagues will give when they get back to Earth. They will say that the universe has no purpose and no plan, that since a hundred suns explode every year in our galaxy, at this very moment some race is dying in the depths of space. Whether that race has done good or evil during its lifetime will make no difference in the end: there is no divine justice, for there is no God.

Yet, of course, what we have seen proves nothing of the sort. Anyone who argues thus is being swayed by emotion, not logic. God has no need to justify His actions to man. He who built the universe can destroy it when He chooses. It is arrogance—it is perilously near blasphemy—for us to say what He may or may not do.

This I could have accepted, hard though it is to look upon whole worlds and peoples thrown into the furnace. But there comes a point when even the deepest faith must falter, and now, as I look at the calculations lying before me, I know I have reached that point at last.

We could not tell, before we reached the nebula, how long ago the explosion took place. Now, from the astronomical evidence and the record in the rocks of that one surviving planet, I have been able to date it very exactly. I know in what year the light of this colossal conflagration reached our Earth. I know how brilliantly the supernova whose corpse now dwindles behind our speeding ship once shone in terrestrial skies. I know how it must have blazed low in the east before sunrise, like a beacon in that oriental dawn.

There can be no reasonable doubt: the ancient mystery is solved at last. Yet, oh God, there were so many stars you could have used. What was the need to give these people to the fire, that the symbol of their passing might shine above Bethlehem?

Some Other Star

Gerald Kersh

'WHEN you travel alone over those plains,' said the dealer in perfumes, 'it is just as well to take a few reliable men along with you. A couple of strong slaves armed with clubs are better than nothing. Me, I should never dream of setting out without a good sharp sword at my side, and a well-sharpened dagger up my sleeve, and a little escort of armed horsemen . . . say three or four. Only the other week we had a brush with bandits on a lonely road. But—'

'Excuse me,' said his host, and left the room. He returned five minutes later, wringing his hands. 'If only she comes through this all right . . . My God, if only she does . . .'

The dealer in perfumes smiled indulgently, and said: 'Have no fear. I was just the same when my first child was born; nervous, excitable. She is young and healthy. You have a good midwife. You are a decent man—you say your prayers, bless God at the prescribed times, and do your duty. Don't worry. Be thankful, rather, that your wife has a sound roof over her and a comfortable bed to lie in.'

'If, please God, it is a son, I shall name him after my father, may his soul rest in peace.'

'Please God it will be a son. And if it is a daughter, then be thankful just the same. A good woman is above rubies. This is a propitious time for a birth of any kind, let me assure you. Did I tell you what happened exactly a year ago tonight? Sit still; keep calm; listen, and take your mind off things for a few minutes.

'You know that I get about a good deal, and know what is going on in the world. So, let me tell you about this time last year.'

From a remote part of the house there sounded a short, sharp cry—a woman's cry. The young man stopped his ears.

'I was travelling,' said the dealer in perfumes, 'to Bethlehem, where I had some little business to transact with a Roman official . . . may worms eat him! The roads were choked with traffic. The population was on the move. Caesar—may he be covered with boils from head to foot!—was taking a census. So we progressed very slowly, for there were thousands of people. At one point I nearly ran down a man and his wife, travelling at less than a slow foot-pace on the edge of the road—an old man and a young wife. I couldn't see her face; it was veiled, but she was riding on a poor old donkey, and it was easy to see

that she was very near her time, poor girl. I made room for them on the road, since it is my custom to be civil to everyone. The old man thanked me very humbly, and led the donkey past. I saw how hopeless it was to try and make progress just then, so I paused, with my little bodyguard, by the side of the road, and sat down to rest and eat and drink a little, since it is my custom never to move a mile without a supply of food and wine.

'It was a clear evening. My men made a little fire. I was prepared to spend the night there, if necessary, since it is my custom always to be prepared with furs and rugs for such emergencies. Good. I was resting there by the little fire when I heard footsteps approaching. My men drew their swords, and cried: "Who is there?" A voice, speaking with a distinctly outlandish accent, said: "Friends", and an extremely queer-looking man came into the firelight. He was, I think, an Egyptian, very richly dressed. It is my custom to notice such things, and I can tell you that his robe alone, sold for half of what he paid for it, would have kept a family in comfort for five years. There were two others behind him—one very pale and the other very dark—not servants, but men like the Egyptian: men of substance, with an air of authority.

'The Egyptian spoke without ceremony. He said: "You are known as Jochanaan the Perfumer." I said: "At your service, my lord. How did you know?" He replied: "It does not matter. We wish to purchase perfumes." I said: "Only too pleased. Wait just one little moment, and I'll show you some very rare articles, gentlemen, at the most advantageous prices . . ." Well, the long and the short of it was that they bought a casket of the finest myrrh, another of the purest frankincense, and a quantity of cassia in an antique jar—without a word, mark you, without a word of argument over the prices—and paid in good Roman gold coin, and turned to go.

'But just before he went, the Egyptian—at least, I think he was an Egyptian—laid a hand on my arm and said: "Your perfumes, my friend, are for the cradle of a King who is more than a King." "And who may he be?" I asked, and he replied: "He will be born this night." "Where?" The Egyptian said nothing but pointed towards Bethlehem, and looked me full in the face in such a way that I felt suddenly uneasy in my inside. Then they went away towards the town, and I spent the rest of the night by the fire, thinking odd thoughts. There was a strange star in the sky that night. It burned after dawn, bright as oil.

'By the morning I was ready to go on. "King," I said, and laughed; then I tested the strangers' money with my teeth, just to make sure. It was quite all right. And so I went into Bethlehem and did my little stroke of business. And then I heard the news.

'It appears that the old man with the young wife was a carpenter called Joseph, of the house of David. He couldn't get rooms in the town, and thought himself pretty lucky to find a stable for the night. And there his wife gave birth to a son. Well, imagine his surprise when, just after the baby was washed, my three strangers came in, and fell on their knees, and laid before the new-born infant the very perfumes they had bought from me the same night. It seems that they had some sign, some omen, some warning, that a Prophet—some say the Messiah—was to be born in such-and-such a place. And the star I saw had travelled in front of them, leading them to the spot. So there you are, my young friend: it only goes to show.

'To most people, a new-born babe is a new-born babe, and nothing more; but that same child may be a prophet, a priest, or a king. So who can tell? The good God may have reserved something special for your first-born, also. Have no fear, therefore. Drink a cup of wine.'

There was silence for a while. Suddenly, the young man leapt to his feet, ran to the door, and listened. The dealer in perfumes, listening also, heard the thin, clear, indefinably woeful wail of a baby forcing out its first breath of air.

The midwife entered. 'Good luck!' she said. 'You have a fine, strong son. And your wife is as well as I am.'

The young man burst into tears of joy, and cried: 'Thank God! Praise God!'

'What did I tell you?' said the dealer in perfumes, smiling with an air of personal accomplishment.

The young man said: 'I shall name him after my father, may his soul rest in peace. I shall call him Judas.'

'Simon Iscariot, accept my congratulations,' said the dealer in perfumes.

The Hollies and the Ivy

Elizabeth Walter

THE house was called The Hollies, the name incised into the stone capping of the gatepost, but it looked as if The Ivies would have been more appropriate, for the word 'Hollies' was smothered under mantling green. Its removal was one of the many tasks the Pentecosts would have to tackle when at long last they moved in.

Gus and Judith Pentecost were a young couple with an interest in interior decor. Gus had recently opened a small shop selling such things as wallpaper, paint, and curtain railing. He wanted his home to be an advertisement for his wares. The Hollies was a double fronted red brick villa with the date 1873 on a stone shield above the porch. It had been empty for years, first owing to a dispute over the late owner's will and then because no building society would give a mortgage on it. It was in a very bad state of repair.

But it had presented a challenge which the young Pentecosts were only too eager to take on. When essential structural repairs had been dealt with, they moved in almost at once. It could not be said that removing ivy from a gatepost was high on their list of priorities, but they would get to it in due course. Meanwhile there was other ivy more loudly clamouring for attention, for the whole of one side of the house and much of the front was thickly covered with it. It was an exceptionally flourishing evergreen; its leaves had a glossy leathern look; its stems were as gnarled and twisted as the veins in an old man's hand. It even obscured several windows, which caused Gus to exclaim angrily that the builders might have cut it back while they were about it.

'They said they did,' Judith said. 'Mr Hardy mentioned it particularly because apparently they'd had such a job. The stems are terribly thick and hard. A knife wouldn't touch them. They even blunted an axe.'

Close inspection revealed that several stems had indeed been chopped through, but it seemed to make no difference. It was an ivy of singularly rampant growth. And near the front door was further evidence of its invasion: two holly bushes stood there, one dying, the other dead. Both were so completely covered with ivy that it was not at first apparent what they were. It was Judith who recognized them and saw in them the origin of the name The Hollies.

Gus surveyed the bushes. 'They've certainly had it now. Nothing for it but to dig them up—if we ever get round to it. The problem here is knowing where to start.'

Eventually they started on a sitting-room, ground floor, on the un-ivied side of the house. They stripped, plastered, papered, painted, laid the carpet and got the curtains up.

'You know,' said Judith, sitting in the middle of the new carpet, 'it's going to be rather lovely when we've got the furniture in.'

'Who says we're going to be able to afford furniture?'

'Of course we shall. We'll buy it second-hand.'

'I suppose you could go round the sale rooms—'

Gus was interrupted by a tapping at the window-pane.

'What was that?' Judith asked.

'Imagination, most likely.'

As if in contradiction, the tapping came again. Together they went to the window. There was nothing and no one to be seen. Yet barely had they turned their backs and resumed their conversation than the insistent, gentle tapping came again. This time Gus pushed back the catch and flung up the heavy sash window. The cold November air flooded in.

'Well, I'm damned! Come and look at this, Judy. It's our clinging friend ivy again. There's a bit growing up on this side and it's tapping against the window. Hand me that knife and I'll soon cut this one down to size.'

' "A rare old plant is the ivy green", ' Judith quoted softly.

'What's that you're saying?'

> 'A rare old plant is the ivy green
> That creepeth o'er ruins old.
> Of right choice food are his meals, I ween,
> In his cell so lone and cold.'

'Sounds cheerful.'

'Oh, it gets even better as it goes on. Something to the effect that he

> 'Joyously huggeth and crawleth around
> The rich mould of dead men's graves.'

Gus closed the window with a bang. 'Shut up and put the light on.'

Judith took no notice. In the same soft, faraway voice she continued:

> 'Creeping where Grim Death hath been,
> A rare old plant is the ivy green.'

Suddenly she shuddered. 'Oh, I'm cold, cold. You shouldn't have had that window open.'

Gus put an arm round her shoulders. 'You shouldn't have dredged up that lugubrious verse. Where on earth does it come from?'

'It's Dickens, believe it or not.'

'It makes one grateful for *David Copperfield*. Come on, let's call it a day and have a drink to celebrate our first victory over friend ivy.'

Next day the ivy was back, tapping on the pane.

Gus now decided on more drastic measures, and took an axe to the main stems all round the house. With great difficulty and several sharpenings of the axe he hacked through them, but two days later it was impossible to detect the cuts. Then he started from the upper windows, endeavouring to tear the plant down from above, but even the smallest tendrils seemed sunk deep into the brickwork, and the tiny roots clung like the suckers of a leech. Perhaps where force had failed, science would triumph. Gus determined to try weedkiller and sought the advice of the elderly man in the local seedsman's, who shook his head when he heard what the weedkiller was for.

'Won't have no effect on ivy,' he prophesied. 'Only thing to do with that is to cut it down.'

'I've tried that and it doesn't work,' Gus said sharply.

'Ah, got The Hollies, haven't you?'

'What's that got to do with it?'

'Quite a bit, I should say. Let's see, The Hollies is the old Dyer place, ain't it?'

'The last owner was a Mrs Dyer, yes.'

'Then you'd expect ivy to flourish rather than holly. It's the female principle, see. The holly and the ivy, like in the old carol. They've been fighting since before Christian times.'

'You seem to know a lot about it.'

'Plants are my business,' the old man said. 'There's a lot of interesting lore about plants if you take the trouble to learn it. The holly and the ivy's an example, see. Once in pagan times they was symbols—male and female, same as the sun and moon. And naturally—' he paused to chuckle—'in any struggle the male—old holly—was the winner. Being evergreens, they got associated with Christmas, but there ain't nothing Christian about them two.'

'What's all that got to do with The Hollies?'

'Why, there it was the other way round. Mrs Dyer, she were the winner. The ivy beat the holly, see.'

'Not knowing Mrs Dyer, I don't.'

'She and her husband—' the old man laid one forefinger across the other—'they was always at it like that, until one day he upped and left her.'

'I don't see much victory in that.'

'She had the house and she had the money, and he were never seen nor heard of again. That's why when she died they couldn't prove the will because he might be living. But I reckon he were dead long since. So did others. So did the police. At least they went round asking questions, but there was never anything anyone could prove. Only the ivy started growing over the holly. Try weedkiller if you like, but you'll never bring it down.'

Gus did indeed try weedkiller, and proved the old man wrong in one respect. Far from having no effect, it seemed to make the ivy flourish more than ever. The normally slow-growing plant was spreading and thickening as if it were a Russian vine.

'It must like the smell of fresh paint,' Judith said despairingly. 'It's half over the back windows now.'

'Either that or it's an exceptionally fertile bit of ground,' Gus suggested. 'We'll have a fine garden some day when we get it clear.'

'*If* we ever get it clear.'

'We'll manage, don't you worry. Some of these weedkillers are slow to act.'

'You can say that again. Look at the way it's growing. I swear this tendril's lengthened while we've been standing here.'

'"A rare old plant is the ivy green",' Gus quoted. 'Isn't that what your poem said?'

'Yes.' Judith suddenly turned and buried her head against him. 'Oh, Gus, suppose it's true.'

'Suppose what's true?'

'That story you told me about Mrs Dyer doing away with her husband.'

'Nothing was ever proved, you know.'

'But perhaps that's why the ivy started growing. Perhaps she buried him here.'

'Seems to me that's a lot of perhapsing,' Gus said uneasily. 'How about: Perhaps you're tired. Perhaps you're letting your imagination run away with you.'

'I might have known you wouldn't understand.'

'Who says I don't?'

'It's obvious.'

'Not to me it isn't. What do you want me to do? Dig down to the foundations in search of a skeleton? Call in a parson to lay an imaginary ghost?'

'No.' Judith shook her head emphatically. 'Just let's get out of here.'

'We can't afford to. We've put everything we've got into The Hollies. You know that perfectly well.'

'You mean we're trapped?'

'Don't be silly, Judy. It's only for a year or two. Until the business gets on its feet. Then we can maybe sell The Hollies at a profit.'

'If it isn't an ivy-grown mound by then.'

Gus glanced at the sitting-room windows. The ivy was well above the sash. Surely it had been lower, much lower, a mere half-hour ago?

'I'll have another go at chopping it down,' he said determinedly. 'And give it some more weedkiller too.'

'You won't do any good,' Judith said, half laughing, half crying. 'Mrs Dyer's going to win.'

It began to look as if she were right. Within a fortnight the ivy had spread to both sides of the house and the front windows were so darkened by it that even on the few bright days of winter, only a little sunlight got through. The Pentecosts slept with ear-plugs to deaden the tapping on the panes. Or rather, they lay awake with ear-plugs. Judith in particular was not sleeping well.

It is possible that others might have noticed the phenomenon of the ivy if The Hollies had not stood well back from the road, behind a brick wall which also had its cloak of ivy and was entered only through a heavy iron gate. Milk and papers the Pentecosts found it easiest to bring with them. Post was left in an old-fashioned postbox, though whether through laziness on the part of the postman or through superstition the Pentecosts were unable to decide. What was certain was that people on hearing their address would say, 'Oh, you've got

The Hollies, have you? The old Dyer place . . .' and their voices would tail away. No one seemed to have known the Dyers, and all enquiries about them proved vain. 'He disappeared,' people would say, 'and she went on living there. Sort of a recluse, she was.'

The Pentecosts, being newcomers, had few friends in the district, and those they had they were anxious not to invite to the house until such time as they had made it a show-place. So no one saw it but themselves.

'Tell you what,' Gus said halfway through December. 'The shop'll be closed for a week at Christmas. Let's have a blitz on the place then. Finish painting the kitchen and lay the vinyl flooring, get the dining-room curtains hung, clear the ivy—'

'Clear the ivy!' Judith laughed hysterically. 'If you think you can do that, you must be mad.'

'OK, I'm mad,' Gus said cheerfully. 'Care to join me?'

Privately he thought Judith looked a little mad. She had lost weight and there were hollows round her eyes which he did not remember. It was more than time they got that ivy down.

On Christmas Eve, stocked up with food and drink for the festive season and with a notice 'Reopening January' on the shop, the Pentecosts rolled up their sleeves and got to work. Towards half past eight when they were at their paint-stained worst, there was a sudden scuffling of footsteps on the gravel.

Judith looked at Gus. 'Who on earth would come here now?'

A moment later a carol broke the stillness, young voices ringing fresh and true in the night air. Downing tools, the Pentecosts unbolted the front door and saw, framed in ivy, a group of carol-singers gathered round a lantern and muffled up as though on a Christmas card. The carol they had chosen was appropriately 'The Holly and the Ivy'. They had obviously been carefully rehearsed. The rendering was far better than Gus or Judith had anticipated. Gus began feeling in his pockets for change.

Realizing that he had left his money in his coat upstairs in the bedroom, he excused himself as the collecting box came round, leaving Judith to thank the singers and enquire their provenance.

'We're a mixed group from various churches,' explained the man

with the lantern. 'We do this in aid of local charities every year. Funny
thing is, we were just going home when someone remembered the old
Dyer place was inhabited, so we thought we'd give you a call.'

'We're very glad you did,' Judith said warmly. 'You sang it awfully
well. I suppose it's because you're tired that you suddenly went wrong
in the last line.'

'Did we?' The lantern-bearer looked blank.

'You sang "the ivy bears the crown", not "the holly".'

'We didn't!' the singers cried indignantly.

'But I heard you. I heard you distinctly.'

They protested that Judith was the only one who had.

She turned as Gus came back with a generous contribution. 'Gus,
didn't they sing "the ivy bears the crown" in the last line?'

Gus slipped an arm round her shoulders. 'My wife,' he explained,
'has ivy on the brain—not surprising when you see how much of it we
have to contend with. But by this time next week it'll all be chopped
down.'

The singers smiled understandingly, sympathetically. 'You've got
your work cut out,' they said. 'Rather you than me.' 'You'll need a
machete for that job.' And then, in a chorus of 'Merry Christmases',
they turned and went away.

Gus closed the door. Judith was white and shaking. 'They *did* sing it wrong,' she said. 'I'm not imagining things. I heard them.' Her voice was beginning to rise.

'What's it matter if they did?' Gus said reasonably. 'They'd hardly admit they'd made a mistake. Holly or ivy—it makes no difference. Have a drink, and then we'll get something to eat. I'm hungry.'

Judith allowed herself to be led away.

No doubt it was because they were tired, but that night the Pentecosts slept unusually long and heavily. Yet when they awoke it was still dark. For a time each lay silent, anxious not to disturb the other. Eventually Judith spoke.

'Merry Christmas, darling. What time is it?'

'Merry Christmas, my sweet. I'll see.'

Without bothering to put the light on, Gus reached for his luminous-dialled watch, a wedding present from Judith, shook it and swore violently.

'What's the matter?'

'Damn thing's gone wrong, that's what. It must have stopped last night at nine-fifteen. Funny I never noticed when I came to wind it up.'

'Well, we can't dial the time because we haven't got a telephone. Does it really take three months to get a telephone installed?'

'Only God and the Post Office can tell you that. I'll go downstairs and get the radio. Sooner or later there'll be a time signal on that.'

Gus struggled into dressing-gown and slippers and went towards the bedroom door. As he passed the window, he stopped as though transfixed, then said in a voice which he tried to make sound normal, 'Here, Judy, come and have a look at this.'

Judith joined him. The window seemed impenetrably dark. Then, as she looked, she began to make out tiny chinks of brilliance, as though there were irregular knot-holes in a shutter. The brilliance suddenly identified itself.

'It's sunlight!' she exclaimed unbelievingly.

With one accord, she and Gus rushed from the room into the darkness of the landing. Frantically they opened door after door. The

whole house was crepuscular and tomblike, though it was a brilliant
day outside. Approaching a window, they stared out at a great mat of
ivy, its woody stems as thick as Gus's wrist, its dark, opaque leaves
overlapping like plate armour. Only very occasionally did a glimmer
of light get through.

Gus unbolted the front door. Where last night the carol-singers had
stood framed in ivy, there was only dense greenery. Gus pushed at it,
but the wall was solid, extending from ground to roof-height; perhaps
over the roof as well. The back door was the same, and so were the
french windows in the dining-room. The house was wrapped in ivy
like a shroud.

It was Judith who put into words the thought they kept trying not
to formulate. 'How are we going to get out?'

'Easy,' Gus said with forced cheerfulness. 'I'll have to chop a way
through.'

'But the axe is in the shed.'

'There must be something in the house that'll cut it.'

'The bread knife, the carving knife . . .'

But it was hopeless and they both knew it. The short day dimmed to dark. The ivy tapped at the windows and scratched like a rat at the door. Towards morning (but of what day when all the days were darkness?) Gus said dreamily: 'Do you suppose that damn plant's getting thicker?'

'Yes,' Judith said. 'Thicker and thicker and thicker. Soon there'll be nothing left of us or of the house.' She began to sing in a cracked and broken voice:

> 'The Hollies and the ivy,
> When they are both well grown,
> Of all the trees that are in the wood,
> The ivy bears the crown.'

'Shut up!' Gus said fiercely, but she went on singing and pretty soon he heard himself joining in. Their voices rose in mournful unison, echoing through the still empty rooms of the house.

> 'The Hollies and the ivy,
> When they are both well grown . . .'

The ivy kept time with them, beating on the window-pane.

A Christmas Tale

John Pudney

THE lion walked through the cold fields all tussocky with frozen mangolds.

He disliked the World War because of the lack of circuses and stale bread (which he favoured soaked in rich gravy). Stale bread was now being saved for swill, and circus business was killed by the black-out. So it was difficult for Smith (that was the lion's name) to practise as a national emblem; and he was driven mad by his conscience because he was not 'doing his bit'. It was therefore with a noble melancholy that he traversed the crisp uncomfortable field and padded through the hedge into Lark Lane. Miss Fond, on her bicycle, nearly collided with him.

'Help! Help! Tigers!' she cried as she dismounted.

'Pardon me, madam, you exaggerate. A *lion*!'

'Lions! Oh help!'

'One lion, madam, at your service,' said Smith; and as an afterthought to put her more at her ease, added, 'and the compliments of the season to you, m'am. These are hard times; but Christmas comes but once a year and . . .'

Miss Fond sniffed. 'I don't believe it. I must have had an accident.'

'I must say I thought you braked rather hard.'

'I don't believe it,' repeated Miss Fond. 'I'm sure I have eaten nothing, nor . . .'

'Nor have I,' said Smith; and his eye, chancing to catch hers at that moment, set her off again crying 'Help! Help!' and making passes behind her bicycle.

'I am hoping to come across a Christmas dinner,' Smith said simply.

Miss Fond, with weak, ungainly haste, leapt back into her saddle and began pedalling like mad. 'I still don't believe it,' she grunted. 'Not a lion! I wonder if I am dead?'

Trotting alongside, Smith remarked: 'You seem very sprightly to me; though, if you swerve about on these frosty roads . . .'

'I don't'—snapped Miss Fond—'as a rule.'

'I know someone who snapped,' growled the lion rather irritably, 'and swallowed more than she meant to.' Miss Fond looked sideways at his noble jaws and pedalled herself almost to death. 'Alive or dead, I shall soon be at the lodge gates,' she panted.

'A lodge, eh!' said Smith. 'With a fine mansion in a park? Nothing would suit me better this Christmas. A place where there is still dignity and repose!'

He frisked with eager anticipation about the speedy but reluctant figure upon the bicycle, causing her to ring her bell ceaselessly to express her alarm.

'You will only make an ass of yourself if you keep doing that,' Smith warned her, as they came to the last lap within sight of the gates. 'And I do not consider it very complimentary to me.'

'His Lordship will pay you all the compliments you deserve,' said Miss Fond, through her teeth, and encouraged no doubt by the nearness of home.

'And who, may I ask, is his Lordship?'

'Lord Trellis, of course . . .' But Miss Fond now observed that the gates were shut. To dismount in the presence of a lion was out of the question. To show alarm by circling outside and crying out was to invite ridicule. Her position as housekeeper at Trellis Hall demanded dignity and an unabated imperiousness.

'That would be Trellis, the big game hunter?'

But Miss Fond saved her breath for a new outcry. 'Gate! Gate!' she cried. 'Open the gates at once.'

Mrs Pleag, her tried enemy these many years, waddled with provocative leisureliness from her lodge.

'Who said *gate*?' said she, knowing very well.

Miss Fond, in a sweat of helpless bitterness, was forced to circle once. 'Don't argue, Mrs Pleag, in the name of God.'

Mrs Pleag stood squarely before the bars like an old-fashioned regiment of the line preparing against an assault.

'I would have you know, *Mrs Housekeeper Fond* . . .' she began, 'that flunkeys, like yourself, there may be up at the Hall . . .'

No more words came from her wide-opened mouth, for it was less than a yard away from that of the lion. She threw her whole bulk against the gate, and her enemy, Miss Fond, plush-faced, with embarrassed energy, swung through, the lion trotting beside.

Lacking imagination as she did, Mrs Pleag decided afterwards, over a strong cup of tea, that the whole thing had been a trick of the light, and that she would say nothing about it to her husband, who, being gamekeeper, would know of any lions—if there were any.

I do not know whether the lion or Miss Fond was the more embarrassed as they approached Trellis Hall.

'A dearth of bread and circuses can lead one into curiously undignified situations,' said Smith, by way of making conversation. 'But no doubt his Lordship is accustomed to keeping a good old-fashioned open house at Christmas.'

'Not with rationing,' answered the housekeeper, with automatic and sour authority.

'Oh! Rationing hardly worries me at all,' murmured Smith, noting with some pleasure the alarm this caused to the bicyclist.

Lord Trellis then observed them with his binoculars from the terrace; and he slapped his great haunches and laughed, and cried, 'Serve her right, the sour old puss; serve her right.'

He was armed only with a 410, which he used for odd potting from the house; and he decided to hold his fire in order to enjoy the pursuit of his housekeeper by the lion, which was a rare novelty, most welcome in the festive season.

'Your Lordship! Your Lordship!'

'What is it, Miss Fond?'

'It's a terrible lion, which has been following me for miles. It keeps snapping, and I'm sure it would have eaten me if I hadn't warded it off. Please shoot it, my lord, before I get off this bicycle. I have already been through so much.'

Lord Trellis stroked his great fibrous whiskers, and mourned the fact that the 410 would not be very effective against the tawny bulk of Smith.

Miss Fond never ceased complaining as she circled in the drive; not did she mention any part of the conversation she had had with the lion.

Lord Trellis, kept very short by her mean housekeeping, suffering from loneliness because he was such a bore about killing big game, and feeling very obsolete in the midst of a World War designed to kill people, if possible as sitting targets, caught the lion's eye, as he rose to hasten to the gunroom.

Smith winked.

Lord Trellis winked back; and seeing that he hesitated about going to the gun-room, Smith remarked: 'The compliments of the season, Lord Trellis. I know I'm intruding, but . . .'

'Don't believe him, my lord,' shrilled Miss Fond. 'It isn't true. Lions don't talk.'

'They get very hungry, though, after running along cold country roads,' said Smith, giving her a look full of meaning.

This made poor Miss Fond circulate all the faster and Lord Trellis to sizzle and boom with laughter.

'Compliments of the season to you, my dear fellow. Come inside and . . .'

'Lord Trellis. I beg you! In fact, I warn you! If that lion enters Trellis Hall, I shall give notice. For years and years I've worked . . .'

But Lord Trellis bellowed and smote himself and boomed back at her. 'Be so good as to ride round to the back door and leave the lion to me.'

'A very good suggestion, if I may say so, my lord,' said Smith. 'As a National Emblem I had hoped to be asked everywhere this Christmas, but I find myself quite on my own resources and . . . '

'Come inside. Come inside. There's the gun-room; there's all my trophies . . .'

That began a very strange Christmas at Trellis Hall.

Miss Fond, who had no intention of leaving whenever she gave notice, because it was much more spiteful to stay on, dismounted her bicycle at the back door, and pranced vengefully into the house.

'His Lordship has got a lion in with him,' she barked at Mr Cod, the butler.

Mr Cod's eyebrows went up and he smiled indulgently, for he had always nursed a suspicion that Miss Fond took a glass of something very strong on the quiet; and he would not, it must be admitted, have been averse to joining her.

'And the cow jumped over the moon,' he said. 'His Lordship has just ordered tea and bread and butter for six; and he says to ask you where is the usual Christmas cake.'

Now Lord Trellis rarely enjoyed himself, Miss Fond saw to that. He revelled in the company of Smith.

They had tea for six. They took down all the dusty trophies. They recalled native war songs and dances. They imitated the cries of animals. They fired shot after shot from the gun-room and lavatory windows. They ate enormously, and fetched up the best port. They made Cod think he was back in the Navy, sent him hollering *avast*, swearing, and skidding in a wild hornpipe throughout the house.

The presence of the lion filled Lord Trellis with defiance. He stamped his feet at Miss Fond and fired revolver shots over her head.

But the presence of the lion—and the looks he gave her—terrified her most.

Never being one who could let well alone, she telephoned the police and said: 'This is the housekeeper at Trellis Hall. His Lordship is with a lion in the dining-room.'

'You mean he is injured?'

'No, he is just talking.'

'*Talking!*' Rich marrowfat police laughter.

She telephoned Dr Luff, and the Clerk to the Rural District Council. Neither of them cared for Miss Fond in any case; and, being convivial, they just laughed. On Christmas afternoon, she cycled down to the lodge, and that was her last extremity.

'Now, Mrs Pleag, you saw me with a lion when I came back on my bicycle.'

Mrs Pleag glanced at her husband, saw him tap his temple and then she said: 'A lion, Miss Fond! Whatever next!'

Miss Fond, bleached with fury, cycled away, and made arrangements for Christmas dinner for eight with exceptional quantities of stale bread.

Smith complimented her upon it. Lord Trellis, who had told him every big game story he knew, said it did her credit and that he would take her on his next safari. Cod sang a song called 'Every Nice Girl Loves a Sailor', and offered her his hand in marriage.

To everyone's surprise, she accepted this; and it therefore fell to Cod's lot to explain to the police, Dr Luff, the Clerk to the Rural District Council, and the Pleags what she had been driving at, which was an almost impossible task, as Smith had gone back to work early next morning.

And lions look so much alike that it is impossible, too, to trace him and get his confirmation of these events—even if he is willing to give it.

A Very Merry Christmas
Morley Callaghan

A FTER midnight on Christmas Eve hundreds of people prayed at the crib of the Infant Jesus which was to the right of the altar under the evergreen-tree branches in St Malachi's church. That night there had been a heavy fall of wet snow, and there was a muddy path up to the crib. Both Sylvanus O'Meara, the old caretaker who had helped to prepare the crib, and Father Gorman, the stout, red-faced, excitable parish priest, had agreed it was the most lifelike tableau of the Child Jesus in a corner of the stable at Bethlehem they had ever had in the church.

But early on Christmas morning Father Gorman came running to see O'Meara, the blood all drained out of his face and his hands pumping up and down at his sides and he shouted, 'A terrible thing has happened. Where is the Infant Jesus? The crib's empty.'

O'Meara, who was a devout, innocent, wondering old man, who prayed a lot and always felt very close to God in the church, was bewildered and he whispered, 'Who could have taken it? Taken it where?'

'Take a look in the crib yourself, man, if you don't believe me,' the priest said, and he grabbed the caretaker by the arm, marched him into the church and over to the crib and showed him that the figure of the Infant Jesus was gone.

'Someone took it, of course. It didn't fly away. But who took it, that's the question?' the priest said. 'When was the last time you saw it?'

'I know it was here last night,' O'Meara said, 'because after the midnight mass when everybody else had gone home I saw Mrs Farrel and her little boy kneeling up here, and when they stood up I wished them a merry Christmas. You don't think she'd touch it, do you?'

'What nonsense, O'Meara. There's not a finer woman in the parish. I'm going over to her house for dinner tonight.'

'I noticed that she wanted to go home, but the little boy wanted to stay there and keep praying by the crib; but after they went home I said a few prayers myself and the Infant Jesus was still there.'

Grabbing O'Meara by the arm the priest whispered excitedly, 'It must be the work of communists or atheists.' There was a sudden rush of blood to his face. 'This isn't the first time they've struck at us,' he said.

'What would communists want with the figure of the Infant Jesus?' O'Meara asked innocently. 'They wouldn't want to have it to be reminded that God was with them. I don't think they could bear to have Him with them.'

'They'd take it to mock us, of course, and to desecrate the church. O'Meara, you don't seem to know much about the times we live in. Why did they set fire to the church?'

O'Meara said nothing because he was very loyal and he didn't like to remind the priest that the little fire they had in the church a few months ago was caused by a cigarette butt the priest had left in his pocket when he was changing into his vestments, so he was puzzled and silent for a while and then whispered, 'Maybe someone really wanted to take God away, do you think so?'

'Take Him out of the church?'

'Yes. Take Him away.'

'How could you take God out of the church, man? Don't be stupid.'

146

'But maybe someone thought you could, don't you see?'

'O'Meara, you talk like an old idiot. Don't you realize you play right into the hands of the atheists, saying such things? Do we believe an image is God? Do we worship idols? We do not. No more of that, then. If communists and atheists tried to burn this church once, they'll not stop till they desecrate it. God help us, why is my church marked out for this?' He got terribly excited and rushed away shouting, 'I'm going to phone the police.'

It looked like the beginning of a terrible Christmas Day for the parish. The police came, and were puzzled, and talked to everybody. Newspapermen came. They took pictures of the church and of Father Gorman, who had just preached a sermon that startled the congregation because he grew very eloquent on the subject of vandal outrages to the house of God. Men and women stood outside the church in their best clothes and talked very gravely. Everybody wanted to know what the thief would do with the image of the Infant Jesus. They all were wounded, stirred and wondering. There certainly was going to be something worth talking about at a great many Christmas dinners in the neighbourhood.

But Sylvanus O'Meara went off by himself and was very sad. From time to time he went into the church and looked at the empty crib. He had all kinds of strange thoughts. He told himself that if someone really wanted to hurt God, then just wishing harm to Him really hurt Him, for what other way was there of hurting Him? Last night he had had the feeling that God was all around the crib, and now it felt as if God wasn't there at all. It wasn't just that the image of the Infant Jesus was gone, but someone had done violence to that spot and had driven God away from it. He told himself that things could be done that would make God want to leave a place. It was very hard to know where God was. Of course, He would always be in the church, but where had that part of Him that had seemed to be all around the crib gone?

It wasn't a question he could ask the little groups of astounded parishioners who stood on the sidewalk outside the church, because they felt like wagging their fingers and puffing their cheeks out and talking about what was happening to God in Mexico and Spain.

But when they had all gone home to eat their Christmas dinners, O'Meara, himself, began to feel a little hungry. He went out and stood in front of the church and was feeling thankful that there was so much snow for the children on Christmas Day when he saw that splendid and prominent woman, Mrs Farrel, coming along the street with her little boy. On Mrs Farrel's face there was a grim and desperate expression and she was taking such long fierce strides that the five-year-old boy, whose hand she held so tight, could hardly keep up with her and pull his big red sleigh. Sometimes the little boy tried to lean back and was a dead weight and then she pulled his feet off the ground while he whimpered, 'Oh, gee, oh, gee, let me go.' His red snowsuit was all covered with snow as if he had been rolling on the road.

'Merry Christmas, Mrs Farrel,' O'Meara said. And he called to the boy, 'Not happy on Christmas Day? What's the matter, son?'

'Merry Christmas, indeed, Mr O'Meara,' the woman snapped to him. She was not accustomed to paying much attention to the caretaker, a curt nod was all she ever gave him, and now she was far too angry and mortified to bother with him. 'Where's Father Gorman?' she demanded.

'Still at the police station, I think.'

'At the police station! God help us, did you hear that, Jimmie?' she said, and she gave such a sharp tug at the boy's arm that she spun him around in the snow behind her skirts where he cowered, watching O'Meara with a curiously steady pair of fine blue eyes. He wiped away a mat of hair from his forehead as he watched and waited. 'Oh, Lord, this is terrible,' Mrs Farrel said. 'What will I do?'

'What's the matter, Mrs Farrel?'

'I didn't do anything,' the child said. 'I was coming back here. Honest I was, mister.'

'Mr O'Meara,' the woman began, as if coming down from a great height to the level of an unimportant and simple-minded old man, 'maybe you could do something for us. Look on the sleigh.'

O'Meara saw that an old coat was wrapped around something on the sleigh, and stooping to lift it, he saw the figure of the Infant Jesus there. He was so delighted he only looked up at Mrs Farrel and shook his head in wonder and said, 'It's back and nobody harmed it at all.'

'I'm ashamed, I'm terribly ashamed, Mr O'Meara. You don't know how mortified I am,' she said, 'but the child really didn't know what he was doing. It's a disgrace to us, I know. It's my fault that I haven't trained him better, though God knows I've tried to drum respect for the church into him.' She gave such a jerk at the child's hand he slid on his knee in the snow keeping his eyes on O'Meara.

Still unbelieving, O'Meara asked, 'You mean he really took it from the church?'

'He did, he really did.'

'Fancy that. Why, child, that was a terrible thing to do,' O'Meara said. 'Whatever got into you?' Completely mystified he turned to Mrs Farrel, but he was so relieved to have the figure of the Infant Jesus back without there having been any great scandal that he couldn't help putting his hand gently on the child's head.

'It's all right, and you don't need to say anything,' the child said, pulling away angrily from his mother, and yet he never took his eyes off O'Meara, as if he felt there was some bond between them. Then he looked down at his mitts, fumbled with them and looked up steadily and said, 'It's all right, isn't it, mister?'

'It was early this morning, right after he got up, almost the first thing he must have done on Christmas Day,' Mrs Farrel said. 'He must have walked right in and picked it up and taken it out to the street.'

'But what got into him?'

'He makes no sense about it. He says he had to do it.'

'And so I did, 'cause it was a promise,' the child said. 'I promised last night, I promised God that if He would make Mother bring me a big red sleigh for Christmas I would give Him the first ride on it.'

'Don't think I've taught the child foolish things,' Mrs Farrel said. 'I'm sure he meant no harm. He didn't understand at all what he was doing.'

'Yes, I did,' the child said stubbornly.

'Shut up, child,' she said, shaking him.

O'Meara knelt down till his eyes were on a level with the child's and they looked at each other till they felt close together and he said, 'But why did you want to do that for God?'

''Cause it's a swell sleigh, and I thought God would like it.'

Mrs Farrel, fussing and red-faced, said, 'Don't you worry. I'll see he's punished by having the sleigh taken away from him.'

But O'Meara, who had picked up the figure of the Infant Jesus, was staring down at the red sleigh; and suddenly he had a feeling of great joy, of the illumination of strange good tidings, a feeling that this might be the most marvellous Christmas Day in the whole history of the city, for God must surely have been with the child, with him on a joyous, carefree holiday sleigh ride, as he ran along those streets and pulled the sleigh. And O'Meara turned to Mrs Farrel, his face bright with joy, and said, commandingly, with a look in his eyes that awed her, 'Don't you dare say a word to him, and don't you dare touch that sleigh, do you hear? I think God did like it.'

ACKNOWLEDGEMENTS

We are grateful for permission to reprint the following copyright material:

Francis Beckett: 'Swiftbuck's Christmas Carol', copyright © Francis Beckett 2001, first published in this collection by permission of the author.

George Mackay Brown: 'The Nativity Bell and the Falconer' from *The Masked Fisherman and Other Stories* (John Murray (Publishers) Ltd, 1989), reprinted by permission of the publisher.

Morley Callaghan: 'A Very Merry Christmas' from *Stories 2* (MacGibbon & Kee, 1964), copyright © The Estate of Morley Callaghan, reprinted by permission Barry Callaghan.

Patrice Chaplin: 'Night in Paris' first published in *Woman's Hour Book of Short Stories 2* compiled by Pat McLoughlin (BBC Books, 1992), reprinted by permission of the author.

Arthur C. Clarke: 'The Star' from *The Other Side of the Sky* (Gollancz, 1961), copyright © Royal Publications, Inc. 1955, reprinted by permission of the author and the author's agents, Scovil Chichak Galen Literary Agency, Inc. and David Higham Associates Ltd.

Margrit Cruickshank: 'Mary's Story', copyright © Margrit Cruickshank 1995, first published in *Chiller* (Poolbeg Press, 1995), reprinted by permission of the author.

John Gordon: 'The Kissing Gate', copyright © John Gordon 2001, first published in this collection by permission of the author.

Dennis Hamley: 'Not Wanting the Blue Cracker', copyright © Dennis Hamley 2001, first published in this collection by permission of the author.

Lesley Howarth: 'The Ghost of Christmas Shopping' from *Quirx: Welcome to Inner Space* (Hodder & Stoughton, 1997), copyright © Lesley Howarth 1997, reprinted by permission of the publisher.

Thomas F. Monteleone: 'The Night is Freezing Fast', copyright © Thomas F. Monteleone 1987, first published in *Masques II* edited by J. N. Williamson (Maclay & Associates Inc., 1987), reprinted by permission of the author.

Chris Naylor: 'The Carol Singer' first published as a Christmas card in *Enigmatic Tales: 3* (Enigmatic Press, December 1998), copyright © Chris Fox 1998, reprinted by permission of the author.

Frank O'Connor: 'The Adventuress' from *The Cornet Player who Betrayed Ireland* (Poolbeg Press, 1981), copyright © The Estate of Frank O'Connor 1981, reprinted by permission of the publisher.

Katherine Paterson: 'Many Happy Reruns' from *Star of Night: Stories for Christmas* (Gollancz, 1980), copyright © Katherine Paterson 1979, reprinted by permission of Penguin Books Ltd.

Alison Prince: 'Josef's Carol' from *A Haunting Refrain* (Methuen Children's Books, 1988), copyright © Alison Prince 1988, reprinted by permission of Jennifer Luithlen Agency.

John Pudney: 'A Christmas Tale' from *It Breathed Down My Neck* (Bodley Head, 1946), reprinted by permission of David Higham Associates Ltd.

Elizabeth Walter: 'The Hollies and the Ivy' from *Dead Woman and Other Haunting Experiences* (Harvill Press, 1975), copyright © Elizabeth Walter 1975, reprinted by permission of the author.

Although we have tried to trace and contact copyright holders before publication, in some cases this has not been possible. If contacted we will be pleased to rectify any errors or omissions at the earliest opportunity.

The illustrations are by:

Martin Cottam:	7, 15, 35, 43, 87, 93, 95, 109, 112, 123, 124, 145, 148, 150
Brian Pedley:	1, 4, 18, 57, 63, 65, 72, 74, 79, 101, 108, 127, 134, 136
Ian Miller:	28, 33, 34, 45, 53, 85, 115, 119, 122
Tim Stevens:	138, 142